A League of Gentlemen

League of Gentlemen Series Book 1

Sharon Johnson

Wicked Words Publishing

Published by

Wicked Words Publishing

PO BOX 712

Hamlin, Pa 18427

Warning:

This book is intended for mature audiences. This book contains material that may be offensive to some people including graphic language, graphic depictions of violence, explicit descriptions of sex, anal sex, male on male sex, oral sex, rimming, frottage, barebacking, rough sex, and a few BDSM elements.

"Where there is only a choice between cowardice and violence, I would advise violence."

~ Mahatma Gandhi

"There is no chance, no destiny,
no fate that can circumvent or hinder or
control the firm resolve of a determined
soul."

~ Ella Wheeler Wilcox

DEDICATION

To my loving, devoted husband and our amazing children, without your constant support, I would have never completed this journey. You have inspired me to reach for my dreams by reminding me that the only failure is not trying.

I want to say thank you for the countless hours my husband helped me brainstorm in the middle of the night, and listened to my constant plot changes when we both needed to be asleep. For all my friends and family who believed in me even when I sometimes lost faith in myself.

To my editors, proofreaders, and beta readers, I would never get anything done without your tireless efforts. It takes a village to publish a book! And my village is fucking amazing.

Contents

Roll Call..1

PROLOGUE 2

Chapter 1..11

Chapter 2..39

Chapter 3..63

Chapter 4..110

Chapter 5..147

Chapter 6..205

Chapter 7..216

Chapter 8..244

Chapter 9..261

Chapter 10..283

Chapter 11..298

Chapter 12..311

Chapter 13..333

Chapter 14..354

Epilogue- 6 Months later 366

Roll Call

Dwayne Simmons, AKA Lucky. Retired Navy Seal current Lieutenant. Hive Sweeper Team One Leader.

Natasha Tsarsko, AKA Shock. CIA Field Agent/Technology Specialist. Second-in-Command.

Steven Arnold, AKA Boomer. Retired Delta Force. Team Sniper.

Keith Pearson, AKA Switch. CIA Field Agent. Lead Groundsman.

Dominic Muccino, AKA Chaos. Former U.S. Marine. Lead Sniper and newest member of the Hive.

Samuel Wright, AKA Sledge. Former Marine. Transportation Specialist.

Dr. Eric Rivers, AKA Doc. Former Force Recon. Combat Medic/Medical Officer.

PROLOGUE

July, Afghanistan Mountains

Staff Sergeant Dominic Ackerman sat patiently in his sniper's nest and waited for his target to appear. Sand burrowed into all his crevices, like a million ants crawling and biting into his skin. The beads of sweat caught the sand and rolled down his back, and it was almost enough to make him want to move.

Almost.

Months of recon had been required to provide this one opportunity to take out one of the most savage terrorist cells in the country. There was no way he'd let a little thing like personal comfort stand between him and the target.

The leader had proved to be an impossible man to predict, and he knew this might be the only chance the U.S. had to stop him. This cell was responsible for fifty confirmed kills; they'd documented their terror campaign from the time their victims were kidnapped until they were beheaded.

Their bodies were often left outside military bases, taunting the soldiers with their brash disregard for human life. As the minutes turned into hours, he alternated with his spotter. Staff Sergeant Sean Harper kept his eyes trained on the compound while Ackerman scanned the roadside.

They were an effective team with more than five confirmed kills even though they had only partnered two weeks earlier. Staff Sergeant Ackerman was thought to be well on his way to beating out Sergeant Chuck Mawhinney, with over eighty kills to his name. Mawhinney was a legend in the United States Marine Corps, with over one hundred kills to his record. Ackerman wasn't sure if the title would be a blessing or a curse.

Hey, buddy, killing sure as fuck beats dying any day, his always-present Angel reminded him.

But even that did little to erase the faces of the men he'd killed, the faces that still haunted his dreams.

He pulled out his rations, which were just enough to get him through the day, and the endless boredom led his thoughts back to all the shitty circumstances that had brought him to this moment in time.

He had had to fight for even his first breath, which had almost been stolen by the umbilical cord coiled around his neck.

Life had seemed out to fuck him since day one, and the rest of his childhood had proven to be just as dangerous. His father had never hesitated to use his fist to display his dissatisfaction with his only son.

He was yanked back into the present when the target appeared just out of range, his training kicking in to shut his thoughts down and focus only on his mission.

Ackerman quickly activated his unit's communication channel. "We have a visual," he whispered into his headset.

Alerting both his spotter and the ground troops ready to seize the compound that he was prepared to take his shot, he had to wait until his target was in the perfect position: one shot, one kill. His mind cleared as his pulse slowed—*breathe in, breathe out, squeeze off between heartbeats.* Five seconds later when the target stepped into the kill zone, Ackerman pulled the trigger and took him down.

"Target neutralized; you are clear to go," Staff Sergeant Ackerman reported before he delivered the second shot.

Armed men stormed from the houses, but with no real target they sprayed rounds wildly out into the desert. A call came over the comm as the unit approached the compound. Ackerman and his spotter took up a defensive position to provide cover fire to the ground team. They let out three-round bursts, effectively neutralizing the combatants.

He watched through his scope as Major Brandon Elliot led his team into the compound to secure the location and deal with any terrorists that still hid in the camp. More enemy targets came from a lower residential building. One by one, Ackerman and Harper took down combatants as they attempted to engage the team.

As quickly as the firefight had started, it was over. With sniper suppression fire from above and direct contact flanked in on all sides, the terrorists had little chance of making it out alive.

In just over an hour, they had cleared the compound of obvious threats. All the women and children were segregated to one group as the older boys and men sat in another to be questioned.

Ackerman and Harper took turns tracking the villagers through their scopes and maintaining visual on the hillside for possible reinforcements. They listened in on their comms while the Major questioned the occupants regarding the locations of any other known terror cells.

One by one, they all denied having any information.

Time slowed down as the Major ordered his men to bring him one of the women, his voice eerily calm as he claimed to have a new way to make them talk. The Major didn't say a word as one of the soldiers dragged the woman in front of him. He pushed her to the ground and fired his weapon. She dropped to the sand. Men and women alike screamed as he sent for another.

"So does anyone know about any more terror cells?" he questioned.

Ackerman was briefly stunned as the Major's translator continued on as if a civilian hadn't just been murdered. "With all due respect, sir!" he screamed into the radio. "What the fuck are you *doing*?"

He had just snatched up his gear to head down to the compound when Harper grabbed his arm.

"Stay out of this, Staff Sergeant. The Major is running the show," Harper growled.

Ackerman yanked his arm away. "Are you fucking crazy?"

Harper's eyes hardened at the question, but he still dropped his hand and stepped back as Ackerman grabbed his rifle. Ackerman was prepared to storm down there and stop the Major by any means necessary. He didn't realize the gravity of his mistake until his partner slammed the rifle's butt stock into the side of his head.

His eyes rolled to the back of his skull as a sharp spike of pain raced down his spine. Before that moment, Dominic Ackerman would have bet his life on the loyalty and integrity of the men he served with. They were Marines.

Honor. Courage. Commitment.

These were the core values of every Marine, or so he had believed until that moment when all his faith had shattered along with his skull.

Ackerman woke up in the infirmary, where it took days for him to piece together the sequence of events that had left him hooked to a ventilator. By the third day, when he had proved he could breathe on his own, the nurses decided to put on his television. At least with that, he had something to compete with the constant beeps of machines. It helped pass the time as he tried to figure out his next move.

Then they turned on the news.

He was being called a hero after a *successful* raid on a compound inhabited solely by terrorists. There were no survivors. After emptying his stomach contents, Ackerman asked the on-call nurse for a MWR (Morale, Welfare, Recreation) line to contact stateside. His first call was to the naval criminal investigators, followed by a long conversation with his old commander.

General Renner was the one person in the U.S. that Ackerman knew he could count on without question. General Renner had been his primary instructor in special operations training, as well as his mentor in SERE (Survival, Evasion, Resistance, and Escape) training, and he knew to his core that this was one man he could trust.

It took less than eight hours for General Renner to have a protective detail provided to his room and ten MPs taking his statement. In the months to follow, he would once again be called a hero for showing bravery by testifying against his former commander and partner.

Time blurred between making that first initial statement and the consequent court martials. The press had been relentless, and, in order to keep his identity from being compromised, Ackerman had been placed on barracks restriction. The only time he left was to be shuttled to and from the proceedings.

Both his former commander and partner received slightly more than a slap on the wrist since Ackerman had not personally witnessed what really occurred after he was knocked out, and the other members of the unit stood behind their commander. Ackerman knew his life in the USMC would never be the same.

He was immediately transferred into a new unit, but the news of his testimony had already spread far and wide. Within the enlisted and officer ranks, he was not seen as a hero. No, he was a buddy fucker: a snitch who had caused both his partner and commander to be stripped of their rank, dishonorably discharged, and sentenced to four years each in prison. He was not a person anyone wanted watching their six, and he couldn't rely on anyone to watch his.

Eight men in total invaded that tiny Afghan village and he was the only one not serving a term in prison. It took two years for him to realize that while he did the honorable thing, his career as a Marine was finished. Unable to find a suitable unit or partner, he was diagnosed with PTSD and given a full retirement.

Now he just needed to figure out what to do with the rest of his life.

Chapter 1

August, Somewhere outside Williamsburg, VA, USA

At zero-three-hundred hours, Dominic stepped outside of his crappy, no-frills hotel and stretched his legs, preparing for his morning run. After leaving the *training farm*—as the CIA called it— he was instructed by his handlers not to go far; he would be rendezvousing with his new team soon.

Soon...

That had been over a week ago, and he'd had more than an entire week with absolutely no contact. He had no idea who he would be meeting with, only that they would contact him. Adjusting his ridiculous fanny pack, he shook off his frustrations and set off at a comfortable pace for his run.

Three miles separated him from the park and trails; the running helped clear his mind as well as give his body something to do while he waited to meet his new team. The air had a frigid bite, but the breeze seemed to wipe away the constant stench of piss that seemed to cling to the city.

He had chosen this time of the morning because the streets were all but dead; he wouldn't have to dodge vehicles or be harassed by other runners on the trails. As he drew closer to the secluded area of the park, Dominic scanned the tree line looking for any hint of danger. Even though there was no one in sight, Dominic had an eerie feeling of being watched.

Paranoid much? his Angel taunted as he picked up the pace.

Years of constant vigilance had his legs moving faster as he scoped out possible hiding spaces. The moment he rounded a curve in the trail that took him completely out of sight of the roads, he was nailed in the shoulder.

Fuck, I'm hit... was his first coherent thought as he swerved to get out of the sights of the sniper. He could tell whoever was firing was stationed high in a tree. But whatever was in that dart was fast-acting. His vision began to dim almost immediately, and it took him a full second to realize he was going to pass out.

He managed to pull his Sig from his holster as he turned to return fire when the second projectile hit its mark. Nausea welled up as he fell to his knees, trying not to vomit as his body fought the effects of the drugs.

As he faded out of consciousness the last thing Dominic heard was a distorted voice's report, "Target is secure. We will be wheels up in twenty minutes..."

Unknown time, Unknown location

Clawing his way back into consciousness, Dominic forced his body to still as he replayed the series of events that had led to his current situation. It all seemed oddly familiar to waking up in that hospital.

He took a mental inventory of his physical condition and was mildly relieved to note that while he was certainly a prisoner, he was more or less uninjured except for the dull ache left from the darts. He kept his breathing even and his heart rate steady; Dominic reminded himself not to fidget.

Struggling will only make the cuffs tighter, his Angel reminded him.

Unable to see his direction of travel through the blindfold, he simply concentrated on the number of turns they made and the sounds he could hear. The two people beside him remained completely silent; if not for the hands that braced him at the corners, Dominic would have thought he was alone.

Well, this must either be our new employers or... the most elaborate set up for an episode of Punk'd ever, his ever-present Angel guessed.

Wiseass.

Only six weeks out of the Marines, he hadn't really been surprised when the CIA had come to recruit him. Being Special Operations made him an asset the government wouldn't want to lose. It hadn't been a hard sale; he only had one unique set of skills, and they were skills that didn't transfer to a nice cushy civilian life.

He was a killer, a HOG—a hunter of gunmen. Trained in the gentleman's game of dirty tricks and dastardly deeds, that was who he was.

He was a predator.

But now, after eighteen months of training and evaluations, he found himself drugged, restrained, and blindfolded—no doubt courtesy of the men he now worked for. Staff Sergeant Dominic Ackerman had died somewhere in Afghanistan as a contractor. At least, that was the story the CIA had created.

Now he was Dominic Muccino, headed towards destination unknown. He would have to be foolish not to wonder if this would turn out to be one huge mistake.

"All right, sweetheart, we're here," said a deep male voice. Dominic could detect the faintest of accents but could not determine the origin. He winced as someone grabbed his bicep, forcing him to turn in his seat.

A second person grabbed his other arm as he was none-too-gently removed from the vehicle. Dominic had to chew back a sudden wave of nausea threatening to empty his stomach as he tried to orient himself to the jerky movements.

Fucking drugs.

Dominic couldn't decide what pissed him off more, getting darted or the fact he hadn't known he was being stalked.

What difference does it make? his Angel asked. *Either way, they made you.*

"Did you assholes really need to sedate me?" he asked once he got his body reasonably back under control. "I volunteered to be here. I would have come on my own," he grumbled.

"All part of the program, sunshine. Don't take it personally. No one ever sees us coming," answered the guy from before. His voice was deep, and his accent subtle and hard to place, but the combination rolled over him like a caress. It kind of made him want to punch the guy in the throat.

Any other time, that voice would have gone straight to his cock, but now, just below the surface, he could hear the taunt that accompanied the words. He made a mental note to kick this guy's ass later.

He was led up a few stairs, across a landing, and into a building. He could hear other people moving around them, going about their business as if the scene playing out was par for the course. After several turns down, leading through what sounded like open areas, he was led into a room where Dominic could just hear a door closing behind him.

It's show time. His Angel snickered unhelpfully.

The men leading him came to an abrupt halt then suddenly jerked back his arms and removed the cuffs. Dominic absently started wiggling his fingers to get the blood moving—maybe he'd get a swing in—as he was directed to move a few more steps to the left.

"Have a seat," a new voice ordered as he was pushed into a chair and his blindfold was removed. Quickly taking in his surroundings, Dominic glanced towards the men flanking him.

Dominic pulled his arm free and spun to face one of his captors, growling, "Touch me again and I'll rip off your fucking arms and beat you to the death with them."

The shorter of the two laughed. "Oh, I'd love to see you try," he said.

His partner chimed in. "Just calm down, and have a seat."

The first man was short and stocky, his brown hair cut into a military high and tight. His posture was rigid, and his face was a mask of neutrality. Dominic pegged him as former military, someone with military bearing. The second man was tall, and despite being seated, he estimated the man's height as taller than his own six-two height.

Dominic sneered at the taller man. "Sit me down," he challenged stepping forward. He was angry and vibrating with the desire to lash out. These assholes seemed to have no issues with the fact that they literally kidnapped him to get him here.

Dominic sized up the other man. He was the total opposite of his partner. He had long blond hair in a ponytail that draped across his shoulder. Most likely a CIA undercover agent. Not only did his stance scream not military, but that cocky, shit-eating grin could only belong to a CIA spy. A spook. The man was sexy as sin and he knew it.

"You do not want to play this game with me, sweetheart," the taller man replied, his face hardening.

Unfazed, Dominic relaxed his shoulders. They might have outnumbered him, but this wasn't the first time he'd found himself at such odds. And those men hadn't fared half as well as they had planned. Dominic's head snapped in the direction of a gruffly cleared throat; he made sure to keep the first two men in his sight.

"Welcome to your new team. We call this place the Hive, Staff Sergeant Muccino. I am Lieutenant Commander Simmons, but everyone calls me Lucky. I'd advise you to go ahead and take a seat," said the African American man who was seated at the conference table. His face stretched in a wide smile.

While his smile seemed open and friendly, his eyes held Dominic's attention. They were dark as night and seem to peer into him, searching, assessing. He looked older, maybe in his late forties, with rich umber skin and his head shaved smooth.

The man's very presence screamed HMFIC—head motherfucker in charge—and Dominic found himself snapping to attention and taking his seat as the man addressed him.

"The two gentlemen behind you are Sergeant Wright and Agent Pearson. Gents, if you would be so kind as to excuse us." Simmons addressed the last part to the now-quiet men still standing behind him.

Dominic watched as the two men silently left the room before turning his attention back to his new commander.

"Now, before I begin, do you have any questions, SSgt. Muccino?" Lucky said.

Dominic schooled his features as Simmons turned back to look at him, to hide both his uncertainties and the anger still simmering beneath the surface.

Dominic's practiced blank expression was like a well-practiced dance to fall back into. Years of hiding every significant part of himself had trained him to bury his emotions, functioning reflexively and just going through the motions to complete the mission at hand.

Lucky

"Yes, sir, I do. Where exactly am I? What type of missions do we work on? I was told that I would be joining a team of specialists. Are they here as well? Will we all be living and training here together? I like to know the men I'll be betting my life on." Dominic rattled off his questions in quick succession, and Lucky wondered if he remembered to take a breath.

It was a common tactic, keeping the new agents disorientated to see how they responded to stressful situations. Lucky had to hand it to this one; if he was nervous, he hid it well. There was only a brief show of nerves before he was able to school his reactions. Lucky was impressed.

Silence stretched out for about five heartbeats before Lucky smiled. "The first part is easy. You are in Pennsylvania. More specifically, you are in a small town named North Jackson in Susquehanna, Pennsylvania. As to your second question, you've just met two of your team members. Everyone else will be gathered for a briefing on an upcoming mission this evening. Our missions are classified. We mainly deal with terrorists operating within the United States."

He paused briefly to allow Dominic a chance to inquire about what had just been shared, but when no questions came, he continued.

"But make no mistake. You have not just joined a team of specialists; you are now in an exclusive league of gentlemen. You were selected for your impressive skills and combat record, and you will find that the others are just as capable. After you get settled in, you will need to report to the armory to select your weapons," Lucky explained.

The look on Dominic's face couldn't be anything other than excitement. Leave it to a sniper to forget that he was pissed by distracting him with the promise of guns.

"Except for your personal sidearm, there are no weapons allowed in the common or training areas, but there is a weapons training facility in a warehouse located on the property. We will be testing and utilizing your skills on this upcoming mission. With your training and number of confirmed hits, you will be taking on the role of lead sniper." Lucky could see the confusion of Dominic's face. New guys never expected to be put on point the first day in.

Lucky again waited a few beats for the FNG— fucking new guy—to process that bit of information before continuing. He had no doubt the young sniper had counted on having a few days to orient himself before he was thrown to the wolves.

But that was not how this group operated. They needed to know right away if he was going to fit the job. He had a good feeling about this sniper. Not only was his record impressive, but he had gone through the CIA training like some kind of wonder kid.

"Wait. I'm going on a mission tonight?" Dominic asked. "With all due respect, sir, I'm not sure how you expect this to go down. Normally I would be given a few weeks with my partner."

Lucky could tell the kid was carefully choosing his words. He might not be in the military any longer, but it was clear he hadn't adjusted to being out. They'd work on that, but for now, Lucky just pressed on with his speech as if Dominic hadn't spoken. Even though he still officially carried his rank of lieutenant, he didn't need the platitudes of military courtesies. This was not the Marine Corps.

"There are three teams stationed at the Hive. Each team normally functions as a separate entity, although we do combine forces for larger operations. All intelligence is gathered by the CIA field agents, but you report directly to me. There are eight members in our team including the two of us. Training is multifaceted: as a battalion, the team, partners, and as individuals. You will find that each member brings a unique set of skills. Your partner will be Gunnery Sergeant Arnold," Lucky stated as he pushed a small sealed package towards Dominic.

There was no doubt in his mind that this kid was a killer, but this was not the Marines or the training farm. They needed to see how he functioned under pressure and if he could adapt and think on his feet. Lucky had gone through his service record the night before, and what some may have seen as a deal breaker, Lucky saw as an opportunity. Dominic had stood up and done what was right even when everyone was against him.

A man of integrity.

And that was the only trait Lucky demanded of his operators.

"Here is the dossier for our upcoming mission. Familiarize yourself with the essentials and your role. The team will meet up at twenty-hundred hours, and any other questions you have will be addressed at that time. Mr.

Pearson will see you to your quarters and give you a general tour. Welcome aboard, Staff Sergeant Muccino. You're dismissed."

As soon as Keith walked in the door, Lucky couldn't help but notice the way he was looking at the new guy. There were no real restrictions placed on the operators regarding their personal entanglements; he just required them to keep it out of the missions and not let it cause any distractions during training.

They were all adults and more than capable to handle their own sex lives. But it still surprised him to see Keith was the first one to set eyes on the man. Keith wasn't known to mix fun with work. No, he would have bet that it would've been Natasha or Sam pursuing the young sniper.

Once it became clear that the two of them were just going to stand there and eye fuck each other, Lucky decided to intervene. He called Keith over to grab Dominic's gear, and he didn't even attempt to hide his laugh as Keith stumbled over himself to move. Not even five minutes in the team and Dominic already seemed to have Keith tripping over his tongue.

Well, watching this little game play out should be fun.

Dominic

The door had begun to open before the words finished leaving the commander's mouth; apparently his escorts had not gone too far.

So that sexy asshole is Mr. Pearson. Just fucking great…

Dominic had the sudden need to stand, as the man who could prove to be his undoing entered the room and their eyes met and held a beat too long. There was a distinct moment of awareness that swept through the room, and Dominic had to hold his breath for a few beats as his new team member looked away and spoke quietly with Lucky.

As he waited, Dominic noticed his palms had started to sweat, and he couldn't remember the last time he'd had to fight so hard to get his body under control. The spook picked up the duffle beside the table and Dominic's eyes were drawn to the way Pearson's pants stretched and clung to his ass and thighs. Dominic's heart rate sped up and his cock hardened as he watched the man move.

God, we are so fucked; with this man, we are completely screwed and not necessarily in a good way, his Angel surmised and Dominic could not have agreed more.

Dominic watched as Pearson swung the bag across his wide shoulders before heading back in his direction. He moved with quiet efficiency; every step radiated power and control. Everything about him showcased that he was a predator, with his muscles coiled tight and ready to strike at a moment's notice.

Damn, this man was just his type. Even though to be honest, he had never actually been with a man outside of a few anonymous blowjobs. But even without the practical experience, Dominic knew he was gay, and he knew what he liked. This man checked every box.

Pearson was muscular without being freakishly large, tall with a natural tan. His face was all hard angles with nothing pretty about him. He wasn't attractive in the conventional pretty boy sense, but he was ruggedly handsome. His face spoke of a man who had lived a hard life, and judging by the wicked scar by his left ear, it had sometimes been violent too. He sported at least two days' worth of stubble that was groomed to outline his perfect mouth.

Sending out the wrong, or in this case right, signal to this man could prove to be an incredibly dangerous move. It was never wise, and it could prove extremely painful, to misjudge a man's preferences. And there was a cold look in Pearson's eyes that said he was a dangerous man indeed.

But danger was not the only thing that seemed to blaze in his eyes. There was also a hint of interest—almost dismissible as a fluke, but Dominic was sure he saw it. He couldn't help but wonder if his commander could sense the buzz in the air.

Squaring his shoulders, his body tensed as Pearson reached out a hand in greeting. "SSgt. Muccino, my name is Keith Pearson, but everyone here calls me Switch. Welcome to the team. We are all looking forward to working with you." His gaze held Dominic captive as his lips curled in a knowing smirk. Dominic noticed that the spook's eyes were a strange mix of blue and gray, like they couldn't decide which color they preferred to be so they had settled on a turbulent shade.

So when the man looked away, as if dismissing him entirely, Dominic couldn't describe exactly how he felt, but he was disappointed and a little unstable. For some inexplicable reason, he desperately wanted that spook to notice him.

Dominic gave himself a mental dressing down, reminding himself for the millionth time that being gay here might not be an option. He was now playing and living in a dangerous world where any sign of weakness could be exploited and used against him. It would be in his best interest to focus on figuring out who the key players in his team were, and who could possibly be a threat, before outing himself.

Dominic had decided when he was leaving the military that if he ever had the opportunity to live an honest life, he would. At the time, it had seemed like an easy promise to make since it had appeared highly unlikely that he would find a man who would want to have a relationship with him. He would gladly come out of the closet for the right man, a partner he could build a life with.

But all he had ever managed were quick pump and dumps, and he was not going to make his life difficult for an off-hand fuck. So as long as he limited himself to casual fuck buddies in the back of bars, there would be no need to tell anyone his taste.

"Thanks, Keith. My colleagues call me Chaos." Dominic returned the brief, firm handshake. Looking around the room, Dominic was annoyed to find that Lt.

Simmons had disappeared from sight without him even noticing.

"Alright, Dominic, or would you prefer I call you Chaos?" He headed towards the door.

"Dominic is fine," he answered.

Keith continued, "I'll show you to your room. Your gear from your hotel has already been packed and delivered."

Dominic followed Keith through a large open area, trying to take in his surroundings instead of openly staring at Keith's ass.

Jesus, man. Get your shit together, his Angel berated him.

Dominic normally maintained ironclad control over his impulses, but this man seemed to be his kryptonite. It was almost like he provoked a Pavlovian response. But getting caught gaping at a man could have unpleasant consequences.

Even though Don't Ask Don't Tell had been repealed, and gay marriage was now the law of the land, the military—as a whole—was still not a safe place for people to find out he was gay.

It's not like home was ever a safe place either, not with Daddy Dearest, his Angel reminded him.

When his father realized he had more than a crush on a boy from school, he had made it known that being gay was not an option. If the beating that resulted in two broken ribs hadn't been enough of a deterrent, the threat of being disowned by his parents had.

Since that day, Dominic had learned to control and hide his desires, keeping up appearances by dating all the local cheerleaders. He had even perfected a method to perform with them sexually, even though seeing a woman naked did nothing for his libido.

If it was only the threat of losing his father, Dominic wouldn't have given two shits; the man had never been much more than a sperm donor and paycheck to him since he could remember. But his mother? For her, he had to be a good son and make her proud. And that did *not* include getting caught with a guy.

Once he joined the Marine Corps, hiding became easier. He had always put being a Marine above his sexual desires, so it hadn't been that hard to mostly abstain. The Marine Corps had provided him with the sense of family he'd never had at home. And when the pressure became too much, it wasn't hard to find some dive off base with a glory hole.

Right out of boot camp, he had been tagged as a Force Recon candidate, having gone through infantry training with the highest marks. In Force Recon, his ability to shoot a rifle had earned him a place in sniper training, and that had been where he'd discovered what he was born to do.

Two years ago, when he'd received the news that his mother had died, and he left the Marines, he'd been left with no real reason to hide who he was. He no longer had to worry about her being disappointed by her gay son.

His father would never be proud no matter what he did, and without his mother, Dominic had no reason to go back. Dominic would always be a *fag* in his father's eyes.

There was no love lost between the two of them. The man hadn't even extended him the courtesy of telling him of his mother's passing. Dominic had had to hear it from strangers.

Dominic had just returned to the farm from one of the CIA's field trips, where the recruits had spent two weeks being interrogated by senior agents. The training evolutions were designed to prepare them for the eventuality that they would be captured.

In the CIA, words like questioning and interrogation were just polite euphemisms for torture. After months of learning the most effective ways of obtaining information and killing their targets, each recruit was given the privilege of experiencing it first-hand.

He hadn't even made it the showers when he saw the familiar uniform of a military chaplain and his training handler heading towards him.

"Dominic, I am Chaplain Roberts. I would like to speak to you in your room," he said.

"Well since no chaplain has ever been the bearer of good news, why don't you just tell me which one?" Dominic asked.

"Which one?" the chaplain started.

Dominic cut him off. Everyone knew what a chaplain visit meant. "Which one of my parents is dead?" Dominic knew the drill.

"Well, if we can just head to your room..." He tried again, but Dominic didn't need to go to the room; he doesn't need to be comforted or hear his words of pity. He just needed to know which one.

Dominic snapped, "Just tell me."

"I am so sorry, but we've received word that your mother died last night. I have informed your trainers; you will be given two weeks of bereavement leave," the chaplain explained.

"I don't need it. Is there anything else?" Dominic asked, eager to get in the showers to wash away the weeks' worth of filth that had found its way into every open pore. After a beat, Dominic said, "Thanks. Please inform my trainers that I will be continuing." The chaplain watched him as he headed to the showers.

Dominic didn't bother to turn around. Anything he had had to say to his parents had been said before he'd set foot on those yellow footsteps.

The memories came back out of nowhere, and Dominic had to take a deep breath to focus on the present. Now that he was working as a mercenary for the CIA he might have a new, even more dangerous, reason to hide.

The world of espionage was dangerous enough without having to worry about his partners turning on him; no, he couldn't risk outing himself until he got to know these people. In the military, he'd had to watch his back because being known as a fag could get him hurt. But these people? These people could probably kill him and no one would ever know.

Hey, buddy, everyone who ever knew we existed already thinks we're shelved in a grave at Arlington, his Angel added cheerfully.

"This is the common area. No outside guests are permitted off the main floor. There is family housing located on the property. You will need your security code to access any other areas. The basement is the situation room; all mission details are limited to that area. All of our tech guys work on that floor with each team having their own specialist. Our technology specialist is Natasha Tsarsko, but she also works out in the field as an operator."

Keith rattled off the names of the different technicians and their skills as they headed towards the stairs. Keith quickly typed in a code and pressed his thumb on the scanner.

"The second floor is the residential area—there is a dining area and kitchen located on this floor. Each room has a private bathroom, and of course you can decorate the space however you want. The third floor is the gym and sparring area." Keith finished his spiel as they stood in front of what Dominic guessed would be his new room.

"This is your room; your neighbor is your partner, Steven Arnold. I'm directly across the hall and next to me is Natasha. I'll leave you to settle in. Let me know if you need anything."

Dominic grabbed the keys rougher than he intended, but he knew he needed to get away from this guy before he said or did something stupid. "Thanks," Dominic mumbled, not even looking back as he opened his door, stumbled inside, and locked himself away in his new life.

He leaned against the door with his eyes closed, trying and failing to get ahold of his thoughts. This had, without a doubt, been one of the single most fucked-up days in his life. First he had been darted and kidnapped by his current employer, then he'd met a spook he may or may not want to fuck, and the cherry on top of this shit sundae was that he'd be expected to perform as the lead sniper on a mission—tonight.

Well, aren't you just a negative Nancy? his Angel taunted as Dominic began to check out his new home.

We've pulled way shitier details than this, so don't go all bitch on me now. Besides, we still gotta find out who the asshole that pulled the trigger is. Getting to punch that jerk in the mouth should make you all warm and tingly inside, his Angel suggested.

Dominic really couldn't argue with that logic. He had a job to do, and task number one was getting to know his new team. The last man Dominic had counted as a teammate had bashed in his skull as his commander had murdered unarmed civilians. There was no way Dominic was walking into another setup.

Chapter 2

Keith stood in front of the closed door for a few seconds as he contemplated the strAngely arousing exchange he'd just had. He had felt Dominic staring at him as they'd walked through the building, so he'd dragged it out, taking him on an extended tour.

Keith had briefly considered throwing the man a sexy wink just to see how he would react, but he'd immediately dismissed that idea. It was not a good idea to hit on the FNG five seconds after meeting him. And the way the man all but ran inside, slamming the door in his face, confirmed that his flirting wouldn't have been well received.

Keith shook his head at his ridiculous train of thought before turning away and heading to his room to get cleaned up.

As he stepped under the blissfully hot spray, Keith chuckled when he tried to imagine how Dominic would react when he found out that Keith was the one who had darted him. He kept the shower brief, just the perfunctory clean up. Stepping out of the shower, Keith briskly dried himself and dressed before pulling his hair up in a messy bun.

He had just walked out of the bathroom when he heard his door being unlocked.

"See you brought the new guy in already. Wanna head down to the range and try out those new assault rifles?" Natasha asked as she stalked into his room. Keith couldn't even be bothered to be annoyed that his partner had simply picked his lock and walked in his room uninvited.

After being partnered together for the last five years, Keith had grown accustomed to her utter lack of respect for anyone's personal space. If he was honest, she was like the sister he never had, nor wanted. They had been paired together after graduating the farm.

At first everyone had assumed their relationship was sexual, but they just worked well together. He had slowly been able to win her trust where few had ever really tried to get to know her.

She was the kind who loved her secrets. Natasha Tsarsko, AKA Shock, was a beautiful, deadly, red-haired mystery. There was little known about her apart from her official records and no one was stupid enough to question her. Her real name, where she came from, and fuck, even her age was classified top secret.

Natasha had shared the fact that her mother was Irish and her father Russian the first night they'd curled in bed with a bottle of vodka as she told him about the night her family was slaughtered. After that, she'd spent years working as an assassin, gaining a reputation as a ruthless killer.

She specialized in taking on cartels, which was what got her on the CIA watch list. Keith understood her need to focus her pain on something. She was beautiful and smart, which was always a deadly combination, but when he added to that her complete lack of remorse, she was a force to be reckoned with.

After defecting to America with sensitive information about the cartel that had employed her, Natasha had been given a new identity. She also happened to be highly trained in electronics and had quickly climbed the ladder with her unquestionable skills with technology.

But it was her ability to kill without a hint of hesitation that truly made her stand out. She killed without empathy; she was a weapon of mass destruction, and when the CIA realized how effective she could be, she was given wide discretion to operate beyond their already loose standard procedures.

"You know one of these days you are going to get yourself shot just walking in people's rooms. Or wanna shoot yourself when you walk in to find me fucking some hot guy through my headboard," Keith groused as Natasha browsed through his magazines on the dresser.

Natasha snorted and laughed as she flung his latest spank mag back on the dresser. "Well, *mladshiy brat*, first you would have to get some hot guy into your bed for that to be of any concern." Natasha had taken to calling him what translated to *little brother* in Russian the instant they met. Keith had been taken back by the gesture, but was quick to embrace their relationship.

Most of their prior handlers had been surprised by their instant connection when they were partnered together. It was an open joke that Natasha was the farm's final test to gauge a soldier's ability to withstand torture. Many of the other agents thought she was a sociopath, but Keith was drawn to a kindred spirit, someone willing to do whatever it took to complete a mission.

"Point made, and very well played," he conceded with a chuckle. "I was planning to go to the firing range, but I have to wait for the new guy to take him down to the armory."

"Hmmm," Natasha sneered. "Yes, and how is our newest recruit? Can't figure out why they feel we need another sniper."

"He's in the room across the hall. Didn't say much but bitch about being darted," Keith snorted, "and you know damn well how Lucky is about partners. Anyway, boss man seems to think he'll be a good fit. Did you get any more intelligence on the guy?"

Natasha rolled her eyes. "His files are completely sealed. All that can be accessed has been fully redacted. Looks like people don't want his past getting out." Keith grimaced, knowing that nothing made Natasha more curious than locked doors.

"Well, I'm sure the Lieutenant knows all there is to know about the guy, and we'll just have to wait until he's in a sharing mood."

Natasha grinned darkly. "That, *mladshiy brat*, is where you are mistaken. This roadblock simply means I have to dig deeper. You know I love a challenge, and it's pointless to try to hide anything from me."

Keith smiled and shook his head. He knew there were few things that Natasha loved more than killing bad people. Hacking computers and building electronic gadgets came in as a close second. But when she was using her gadgets to kill people, the joy she got from that was truly scary—in fact, it almost seemed to make her giddy. Though in this case, Keith was more than a little interested in her target. Yes, he too would like to know more about their new elusive teammate.

"Since I know there is no talking you out of it, I'll just tell you to be careful. If his file is buried that deep, then it stands to reason it is being watched and any attempt to access it will be noticed," Keith warned, but he could already see in her face that the game was indeed on.

"Yes, little one, you know me well. I am going to work on my programs. Call me when you're ready to hit the range," Natasha said fondly before heading to the door.

Once Natasha left, Keith was able to completely focus on the upcoming mission. It seemed as if he was going to be up first to pair with Dominic. Lucky insisted that each agent spend time working together; not only did that practice help build unit cohesion, it also ensured that the team could regroup with little to no warning and still be effective.

Dwayne Simmons, AKA Lucky, was their lieutenant and team leader. After twenty-five years as a Navy Seal, he was transitioned into the CIA during his last year of enlistment. In addition to his intimidating presence, his massive bulk on his six-foot frame was enough to make most people cower. But his dark eyes, skin—with its unmarked perfection—and killer smile worked as a complete contradiction to his tough-as-nails persona.

Although he pushed the team to be the best, he approached his role as leader by being the protective father figure. Everything about the man screamed top dog; without abusing his authority, he simply took command without any posturing. He commanded respect and total loyalty; when they had first met, Keith couldn't help but obey his overpowering dominance.

Keith headed down to the main floor to fill out his after-action report and account for the sedation darts. It was standard after any mission if there was any type of contact, even the non-fatal kind. He also needed to return the rifle to the armory from the safe downstairs, but that could wait until Dominic asked to go.

"Hey, wait up, Keith," Sam called out as he jogged to catch up.

"Hey, my man." Keith held the door so Sledge could follow him inside.

Samuel Wright, AKA Sledge, was the official transportation specialist. If it moved, he could drive it. From helicopters, to planes, to tanks, and everything in between, Sam could get the team anywhere. His talent for liberating vehicles led Keith to believe that he had some not-so-legal training as well. Sam also held the dubious honor of being one of their go-to seducers; being bisexual, he had no problem getting close to any gender to complete the mission.

His jaw-dropping good looks disarmed everyone he trained those sexy brown eyes on; his rich Puerto Rican accent left broken hearts in his wake. With over a decade as an infantryman in the Marine Corps, he was as deadly as he was beautiful. Keith had struggled to keep his hands off the well-versed player at first, but now he considered the man just another one of his brothers.

"So what did you think?" Sam asked with a look that could only be described as predatory.

"Think of what?" Keith hedged.

Sam looked at him as if he had grown a second head. "The new guy, Dominic. What did you think?" he asked again. Keith had to resist rolling his eyes.

"Well he didn't say much more after you left, but you saw his kill record; I'm sure this guy is the real thing."

This time Sam rolled his eyes "The fuck? Who cares about his kill record? I'm talking about how fucking hot that guy is. I had to mentally beat down my dick the whole time we were standing in front of the Lieutenant."

"That's because you, my friend, are a complete slut. But no, I did not fail to notice his good looks." Keith didn't exactly know why Sam's comments were grating on his nerves, but he did not like the gleam in the man's eyes. "Anyway, you have no idea if he swings that way. It could be a fatal mistake to push up on a man that could drop you from a mile away." Keith hoped that he was successfully pulling off a look of nonchalance even though he had the uncontrollable urge to warn Sam away.

"Well I wasn't planning on asking him to suck my dick right away. But I was hoping you got some kind of feel of him during the tour," Sledge continued, apparently unaware that every single word out of his mouth about Dominic was testing Keith's patience.

"Nope, he didn't say much," Keith said briskly. "Did you finish your after-action report?" While he wasn't sure if that was a spark of interest he thought he saw in Sam's eyes, or even if it would lead to more than a casual interest, he knew he didn't want to chance Sam getting his hands on Dominic.

"Nah. That's what I was headed to do right now," Sam answered, and Keith was relieved that the subject of Dominic was dropped, at least for now.

Keith considered slitting his wrists as they sat and went through the mind numbing paperwork that needed to be filed.

Gotta keep the paper-pushers happy.

Keith and Sam filled the lull of the day discussing the upcoming mission. Natasha had said that there were new developments that would have to be dealt with. He had no idea what last-minute changes Natasha was working on, but they went through the logistics of potential escape plans in the off chance things went sideways.

"My main concern is all the men the target travels with. If anything, they will be the greatest threat," Keith admitted.

The conversation stalled when Sam said, "That's the problem of dealing with the mob. They have kids lining up to die for them while they're still in high school. I wonder how Natasha feels about taking out some fellow Russians—" He stopped mid-sentence, staring blankly at his stack of papers.

Keith couldn't figure out what Sam was even suggesting. There was a reason Natasha had earned her moniker SHOCK—Scarlet-Haired Ovulating Commie Killer—she almost seemed to take pleasure in eliminating Russian mobsters. Keith knew why, but it wasn't knowledge he'd ever share with anyone.

After a few seconds of silence, Keith glanced over at Sam, hoping his face conveyed a look of, "well, go on…"

When it became obvious no further comment would be forthcoming Keith asked, "What? Don't you think she's up for the task?"

Sam grimaced, startled, as if he hadn't realized he'd spoken out loud. "Um, no, it's not that. It's just that she has no love for good ol' Mother Russia, and I wonder what she feels when she is tasked with killing one of them."

"Sam, believe me when I say, when it comes to killing anyone that has done half the shit these shit bags have done, Natasha gives less than zero fucks about taking their life," Keith answered easily.

Very few agents knew what hells Natasha had survived in Russia; almost everything most people knew about her past was a fabrication. Except for a select few, no one knew her age, hometown, or even her real name. When Natasha finally opened up and told Keith about her past, so many of her strange behaviors suddenly made sense.

It explained why she was so guarded and secretive; her explosively violent tendency to protect those she cared for was a trait carved into her at a very early age. She had learned how to harness all that rage and pain she'd been left with and channel it into her work.

Even without knowing all of that, Sam nodded his agreement. "Yes. Natasha is crazy scary when she is taking down her prey. Although, watching her at work does get my dick hard…" he joked, wagging his eyebrows comically.

Keith laughed. "Dude, what doesn't get your dick hard?"

Sam looked as if he was seriously considering the question before he shrugged his shoulders.

"What can I say, I have a high sex drive," Sam finally conceded, going back to his paperwork.

After Sam turned in his report, he immediately left to take care of the transport vehicles for the night's mission; as the team's designated driver, he was also tasked with maintaining the entire fleet of vehicles.

Keith finally finished up his own report. Deciding to get his blood work done while he was already there, he made his way down the hall to the infirmary.

"Hey, Eric. I'm here for my blood draw," Keith said as he entered the office.

Eric looked up from the many charts on his desk, obviously stunned that he hadn't had to chase Keith down this time. Keith bit back a laugh, not wanting to taunt the doctor into taking his time with the needle. The man could be downright sadistic when he wanted to be.

Dr. Eric Rivers—AKA Doc—was the team's combat medic. Having served with Force Recon for ten years, he was as capable of taking a life as he was saving them. Having served in the Navy for ten years while he pursued his medical degree, he had been promptly transferred to the Marine Corps.

There he had served with special operations, where he'd learned how to be an effective operator, capable of holding his own on the battlefield. Eric may have been forty-two, but his age was well hidden by his mixed East Asian heritage, and he instead sported boyishly good looks.

Eric

Eric pointed to the table and gathered his supplies; being the medic required him to not only patch the team up in and after field work, but to maintain their baseline health as well. These were very expensive pieces of government equipment, and he was tasked with keeping them functional.

No matter how big and dangerous these guys were, they all seemed to turn into giant pussies when it was time for a needle. Keith was no exception as he eyed the exam table like he expected to be impaled.

"How nice of you to come in on your own. Take a seat and roll up your sleeve," Eric said.

"Yeah, figured maybe you'd give me a sticker if you didn't have to chase me down this time."

"Or I could just get Natasha to dart you next time. Maybe slip a little something in your drink," Eric countered. This was not his first time at the dance. He had his ways to keep the men under his care compliant.

"You truly are a cruel, cruel man," Keith complained but took a seat on the table and rolled up his sleeve.

Eric swabbed the area quickly; he still needed to get the rest of the team through the lab. With a new team member on board he would need to start a new file, as each operator had an RFID chip inserted into their body. This allowed the Hive to always be able to locate their operators. In the past, when undercover agents were captured, the agency had no way to locate them until their body was found.

The world of espionage was fraught with dangers, and the greatest for any agent was having their cover blown. It took a lot of hard work and sometimes years to cultivate the identities they used in the field. Losing one had significant consequences.

"So you got to do the hit on the new guy. How'd he take that?" Eric asked as he efficiently inserted the needle into a vein.

Keith flinched and pulled away, dislodging the catheter. Eric fixed him with a glare as he tightened his hold on Keith's arm.

Keith grimaced, asking, "What?" when Eric had to pull back and reinsert the needle.

Keith

Caught off guard, Keith jerked his arm inadvertently. It sounded like Eric was asking him if he was hitting on the new guy. "What?" he asked cautiously.

"The new guy. I heard that you were the one who darted him. How did he take that?" Eric specified, although he arched his brow in question.

"Yeah, he doesn't know who darted him yet, but I can tell you he has very definite opinions about it." Keith tried to cover his blunder with a self-deprecating laugh. "But it was a clean shot."

"Well, I'll get to see your handy work when he gets his tags." Eric laughed while he covered the tiny prick mark with a heart-decorated Band-Aid. Keith's lips quirked up.

"I don't even want to know where you find these things, Eric." Keith just shook his head at Eric's indignant look.

"Well, I do what I can to keep your inner princess happy, Keith," Eric deadpanned. Keith tried to stifle his grin at his friend's flippant response, but it was useless.

Keith gave in and let out a bark of laughter as he left the room.

He continued to hear Eric's deep-throated laugh even after he closed the door. He needed to turn his reports in to the Lieutenant and grab chow before it was time to head to the range. The analyst section was closed off when he passed, with their *do not disturb* message pasted over the frosted window. He would have to call Natasha to see when she would be free; being the most senior analyst, she was no doubt chest deep in whatever had them closed in.

Natasha answered after the first ring. "Sorry, Keith, I won't be able to head to the range. There have been a few last minute changes to tonight's mission, and I need to get my toys ready," she said hurriedly.

Keith could hear her tapping away at the keys of her computer as they spoke. He had learned after years of partnership that once Natasha was in her electronic warfare mode, there was no use trying to get her attention.

"No worries. Is there anything I can help you with?" Keith asked even though he knew the answer was no.

Even if one day she said yes, Keith doubted he would have the slightest clue what she was doing. This was her nerdy super power; though she was deadly in the field, her ability to build spy gear was bar none.

"No. Just grab the new guy and head down without me. I'll catch you in the briefing," she mumbled distractedly before ending the call.

Keith blinked, looking at the phone in his hand; somehow he was a little surprised by Natasha's cold detachment when she was focused on the job. Brushing it off, Keith headed back to the main meeting area.

He supposed he should head up to his room and wait for Dominic to find him once he finished settling in. The smile that crept onto his face at the thought of seeing Dominic was the first hint that Keith would have to be careful around him.

Steven Arnold—AKA Boomer—the other sniper of the team, was laughing with William, a young agent from team four in the movie room. Steven was the oldest member on Keith's team other than the Lieutenant; at forty-three years old, he had already retired from the Army. He had served on Delta Force as a sniper and explosives expert for twenty years.

At barely five foot ten, he had a slight, muscular build and was often overlooked. He was normally quiet and reserved, which was an excellent cover that allowed him to get close to his mark. He carried himself in a manner that didn't stand out in any way, but when he did strike, his prey never saw him coming.

"What's good, Steven?" Keith asked, nodding a greeting to William. The younger agent returned his greeting before saying he needed to bag off for some training evolution.

"Everything's good, my man. I'm living the dream!" Steven answered. "How about you?"

"Same. You been up to meet your new partner yet?" Keith asked, eager to hear his assessment of the new guy.

"Nah, heard he has a temper," Steven drawled around a grin. Gossip spread through the Hive faster than an old ladies' bridge club. It wasn't surprising that Steven had heard about Dominic's indignation at being darted.

"Yeah, you can say that," Keith agreed. Even though he'd been at a clear disadvantage, Dominic hadn't just bristled at his captors. He'd glared at them with a look that promised retribution.

Not that he would admit it to anyone, but it had hardened his cock when Dominic had leveled his pissed-off gaze at Keith. No doubt the two of them would have gone to blows if the opportunity had allowed it, but that reaction had Keith fantasizing about blowing in an entirely different manner.

They chatted for a few minutes about the latest training evolution and vaguely about the upcoming mission. Steven mentioned another seasoned agent who stopped in to see the boss today while Gerald bitched to anyone who would listen about his new partner.

Keith wasn't all that surprised to learn that Gerald had scheduled an interview with Lucky to discuss transferring over to team one.

"Rumor has it his current partner is a homophobic ass, and Gerald damn near knocked his teeth down his throat when the guy said Gerald couldn't be mad that his wife didn't want to be married to a guy that liked to suck dick," Steven said in a hushed tone.

"He what? I'm surprised that Gerald didn't kill the fucker," Keith stated.

"Yeah well, what it did do was have him pulled out of the field. No one is dumb enough to try to put those two back together, and Gerald has to wait for the official dressing down from Washington," Steven said and Keith sighed deeply, annoyed. "He's being run up because he checked that guy?"

Steven nodded in agreement "Yeah, but that's what happens when you put your partner in the hospital. No matter how badly that ass kicking was needed, the higher ups are gonna have to do something, even if it's just for appearances."

Keith nodded; he really couldn't say anything to that. The CIA was pretty forgiving for what their field agents got up to. But that didn't extend to said agents putting others in the hospital. Keith decided to speak to Natasha privately about Gerald. He didn't really know the other agent, but no one should have to put up with shit like that.

After a few barbs back and forth, Keith made his excuses to leave. He needed to be available for when a certain sniper went in search of his hardware. Most snipers seemed to have what Keith considered an unhealthy connection with their weapons. It was almost sexual; many of them would let him fuck their girl before they'd let him touch their piece.

So he had little doubt that Dominic would be looking to get his babies back sooner rather than later.

Chapter 3

After quickly stashing the small amount of gear he traveled with—someone had boxed and brought everything from his hotel room—into various drawers and the lone closet, Dominic took the opportunity to really appreciate his new accommodations.

He also made a mental note to find out who went rummaging through his shit. Not to cause problems; he just wanted to know.

And maybe break a few fingers? his Angel was quick to add on.

To say this was a step up from the barracks and the dinky hotel rooms he had called home would be a gross understatement. Everything in the space seemed to be made of heavy oak. It seemed as if the CIA spared no expense when it came to setting up an operations location; this entire place was huge and his room was larger than most apartments.

Well, well, well. Looks like we are finally stepping up in the world, his Angel sing-songed in the back of his mind.

A large desk sat in front of what had to be a bulletproof window looking towards the road. There was also a comfortable-looking blue loveseat and wood bookshelf against the far wall. The most impressive feature, however, was the large king-sized bed.

The ornate frame and headboard dominated the room without making the area seem closed in. Dominic took note of personal touches he could give to the space, although he wouldn't need much. This was honestly the nicest place he'd ever lived in.

Unsurprisingly, the bathroom had the same kind of flair. The fact that he had a single room was more than Dominic had ever hoped for, but this private en suite almost made up for him being darted. There was a single-person Jacuzzi tub, and by the looks of it he'd have room to lie back and stretch his legs. The shower had more knobs and levers than a joystick, but he was sure he'd have plenty of time to figure it out.

Hey, it could even fit two as long as you two don't mind standing real close, his Angel leered.

Dominic had to laugh at himself; not even a day in, and he already had a situation. The only reasonable response he could come up with was to avoid Mr. Keith Pearson at all costs.

Stashing away his hygiene kit in the bathroom, Dominic decided to skip shaving. He wanted to head to the armory as soon as possible. No doubt his sidearm had been secured there after they sedated him. The only problem was that Keith hadn't mentioned where the armory was, or how he would even get in the building.

Hell, the stairs leading to the living area had a coded and fingerprint-enabled lock, so there was little chance he'd gain entrance to the armory with only his witty disposition and a smile.

Hey now, speak for yourself, buddy. My charms have been known to get us in and out of some tight places, his Angel interjected.

That left him with only one option, an option that went against his earlier plan of avoidance. Leaving his room, he hesitated to knock on Keith's door. Although he didn't look forward to being around the guy, he had no idea where anything was located outside of this building.

Look, the guy said he was available if we needed help, his snide Angel reminded him.

Dominic liked to think of that little voice in the back of his mind as his guardian Angel. Listening to that voice had saved his ass on more than one occasion, but it didn't mean that voice wasn't a dick most of the time. *Fuck it. I need his help.*

Knocking on the door, Dominic took a moment to shove his lust down, way down, into the deepest corner of his mind. "Let me guess: you want to check out the armory. Go get your guns?" Keith said by way of greeting as soon as the door opened.

Dominic blinked. "Yes, I need to go by the armory to get them and check out a rifle." He paused again to gather the brain cells that had scattered when the man flashed a small grin at him. "I wasn't sure how to get there or if I'd be able to get in," Dominic continued.

Keith grabbed a jacket from somewhere behind his door. "All right. I'll drop you off at the armory on my way to the range. Remember, no firearms in the common areas, but you can keep your private piece in your room."

"Yeah," Dominic added lamely. It looked like he could mark off the ability to speak in complete sentences around this guy.

They had made it almost out the door before Keith spoke again, asking, "So how'd you like your room?"

"Good," Dominic answered, wincing as he once again managed to sound like an idiot. Keith, however, must have found the way he was stammering at least funny, as the corner of his mouth twitched up in an almost smile as they walked outside.

Dominic could feel the heat rising in his cheeks as they made their way outside. He knew his blush had to be visible, but there was no way of hiding the effect Keith was having on him.

"Good. So are you normally a man of few words unless you're threatening to rip off people's arms or is this an off day?" Keith 's voice tilted back into that unknown accent. Dominic refused to even attempt a witty reply and chose to just grunt in what he hoped would be taken as confirmation.

Keith

The walk to the armory was tense—Dominic tailed behind him in near silence, one word answers or grunts his only replies—but Keith felt Dominic's eyes on his ass the entire way, and the blush that kept creeping up his face was adorable.

"Here we are," Keith said, purposely stopping short. Dominic must have been getting quite the eye-full, seeing as he ran into Keith's back.

"Fuck, sorry, dude," Dominic said as he nearly stumbled, trying to keep their bodies from pressing together.

Keith just waved him off; he didn't feel the need to point out the blush that had crept further up Dominic's throat and rapidly spread to his ears.

"They will be expecting you. You'll be able to get a locker while you're here. Not to mention they have a section of rifles I'm sure you'd be interested in checking out."

"Thanks, man," Dominic said with a wave.

Keith watched him go, waiting until Dominic turned toward him again before throwing him a wink. The results were instant: Dominic's face paled and he spun and stomped his way down to the armory. Keith laughed out loud.

By the time he made his way to the shooting range, Natasha had already finished her run and was policing her shells. Two other agents were at the indoor, six-lane firing range. Each person secured their weapon as the red lights flashed, signaling the shooters of his arrival.

"So you finally made it," Natasha drawled as she walked up.

"Yeah. Thought you said you weren't coming? Besides, I just got back from taking the new guy to the armory," Keith said, loading his DE50 Desert Eagle Mark XIX pistol. He was not as obsessed as some of the other people he worked with, but he never skimped on the quality of his sidearm.

Natasha shrugged. "Wasn't gonna until Lucky pulled everyone out to go over the op. Spending time with the new guy, huh? What's the assessment?"

"Hard to say. He's still a bit pissy about being darted, so we didn't have any bonding moments," Keith chuckled. It wasn't the only thing he noticed about Dominic, but that was all he wanted to disclose at the moment.

"Men," Natasha sneered in her usual tone. "You are all so fucking whiny. If being darted is the worst thing that happens to him, it'll be a miracle. Did you tell him it was you that pulled the trigger?"

"Of course not," Keith said, inserting his ear plugs and motioning for Natasha to take her lane. He would deal with the fallout of that later; for now, he just wanted to clear his mind.

Dominic

After retrieving his nine-millimeter Sigs from the armory, Dominic headed straight back up to his room. The process to retrieve his side piece was remarkably easy, but he was still rattled by his last interaction with Keith.

Specifically, what was up with that fucking wink? He'd spent the entire time in the armory going over every word exchanged between them, and he still knew nothing.

Dominic decided that nothing would be gained by dissecting something that could be explained away as just being friendly. Stewing over it was asinine and unproductive. Besides, he'd be expected to shoot tonight, and he'd be lying if he said he felt at the top of his game. Luckily, the drugs seemed to have even dampened his Angel's quick tongue. He eased onto what had to be the most comfortable mattress in the world.

After his nap—*damn, that makes us sound old*—he headed towards the kitchen to grab a snack before the briefing. He could hear a lively conversation with several distinct voices as he headed down the hall and once he realized he was the subject of debate, he hesitated before reaching the doorway, careful to stay out of sight. *Nothing like being the FNG*, his Angel quipped.

"No need to be shy. We already know you're out there," a rough voice called out, the accent thick, throaty, New York, and with a Hispanic flavor.

Huh, thought we were a little stealthier than that, Dominic's Angel criticized him, and he chuckled to himself as he strolled into the large room.

That was one of the problems with being surrounded by highly-trained professionals; he rarely got the drop on them. They were always scanning the area, looking for the next threat. Standing in a semi-circle were three men and one remarkably beautiful woman.

"And you must be Dominic. Good to meet you," said the Hispanic man as he offered his hand. "My name is Samuel; everyone calls me Sledge or Sam. I am sure you remember me from earlier. And these are my esteemed colleagues Natasha, Eric, and Steven."

Dominic gave a quick nod to each person as he was introduced. No one smiled; no one spoke. They just watched him carefully as if they were looking for flaws.

Turning to study his new partner, Dominic noticed Steven didn't seem to be overly happy to meet him.

Well, who the hell likes to meet the new guy who is about to be your boss? his cynical Angel huffed.

Well, tough shit. If this guy thinks he can intimidate us, he's in for a rude awakening, he told his Angel.

"So you're Gunnery Sergeant Steven Arnold? Looks like we will be teaming up," Dominic stated as he held the man's gaze, tense seconds passing as neither man looked away.

Hey, let's just pull out our dicks. It will be quicker to prove who's the top dog than this stare down, remarked his helpful sidekick.

Finally, Steven held out his hand. "Seems so. We're all about to eat. Wanna sandwich?" he drawled in a heavy southern accent.

The female agent—*Natasha,* his Angel helpfully supplied—was already throwing him a plate when he answered. If he hadn't been quick, she would have nailed him in the face. "Yeah, thanks. I was coming in here to find some chow."

"Soda and fixings are in the fridge. By the way, everyone calls me Boomer," Steven rumbled as Dominic moved past him.

"Thanks, Boomer. My unit called me Chaos," Dominic replied while he grabbed the condiments and a drink, then he took a seat.

Natasha clapped her hands together, motioning to him and Steven. "Well, now that you two boys have finished your mating ritual, perhaps we can finish eating." Natasha laughed at her own joke as she went to fix her plate.

Apparently, everyone took her suggestion as a command and went back to their lunch. Dominic wasn't sure why, but something was nudging at him, telling him to not let his guard down around her.

While the conversation stayed lighthearted, there was definitely something about the way Natasha looked at him that suggested that she would be one of the gatekeepers between him and being accepted as part of the team.

No worries, pal. We'll just dazzle her with our winning personality! his Angel supplied helpfully.

As each person joined him at the table, their friendly banter continued. He spent time getting to know his new team members, but too soon, Dominic headed back to his room to grab a shower before the briefing. Even though they all seemed to be waiting to pass judgement, Dominic could tell the members were close knit.

He threw himself across his bare mattress and grabbed the mission file. There was a package of standard-issue white bed sheets, along with what would undoubtedly be the world's itchiest blanket, laid out on the dresser, but he would deal with that later.

Ripping open the envelope, Dominic was surprised when there were only two documents inside. They were light on information other than his specific role. According to the dossier, he was to dress for a night at the clubs.

Keith

Keith looked at the clock on his nightstand as he pulled on his clothes fresh from his shower. There was still time before the briefing at nineteen hundred hours.

Time seemed to have slowed down to a crawl since he had first seen Dominic Muccino through the scope of his rifle. Even with the angle and distance he'd been from his target, Keith could say that the photo in the man's file was a disservice to how handsome the man was in person.

Keith had no misconceptions about his appearance. He intimidated almost everyone he met, but this guy seemed to have a different reaction to him entirely. While Keith was at least ninety percent sure the man was interested, he was one hundred percent sure Dominic was either in the closet or didn't even realize he was gay.

After the last farce of a relationship he'd had, Keith had vowed that he would never go back into the closet to be with a man who wanted him to be a dirty fucking secret. Being openly gay in the CIA had not been easy; he'd had to fight almost nonstop to gain the respect of his peers.

His family had accepted him being gay readily, but in a field where masculinity was prized, he was often seen as a threat. Growing up in and around the Israeli army had taught him how to fight.

When he'd told his parents at thirteen that he was gay, his mother had cried as she hugged him and said they loved him no matter what. His father had doubled his training, telling him he loved him too much to leave him vulnerable in a world where people might not accept him.

He had sworn after the last time that he wasn't getting involved with anyone who wasn't looking for long-term. To that end, he had all but remained single for the last two years, waiting to meet the man he would spend his life with.

But none of those vows stopped Keith from fantasizing about Dominic as he stood in his shower; his cock throbbed as he imagined those perfect lips wrapped around his dick. Giving in, he quickly grabbed the shampoo to lube up. Gripping himself firmly, he began a slow pull from root to tip as he leaned his head against the wall.

Remembering how Dominic's skin flushed had him quickening his pace as he fucked up into his hand. He pictured Dominic's large hands stroking his cock and that strong-looking mouth taking him down to the root. The man's body seemed perfect, and his firm ass in those running shorts had almost made Keith miss his shot. He twisted his wrist once he reached his sensitive tip, his orgasm racing down his spine.

Gently rolling his sac with his free hand, he slowly trailed down his perineum. He quickened his pace as he imagined how it would feel to have Dominic's rough hands slide down his ass, using one finger to gently circle his hole. Keith let his finger ghost over that puckered flesh as his mind pictured someone else teasing him open, while picking up the pace with the other hand.

Keith imagined burying his hands in Dominic's short brown hair as he fucked his throat, those perfectly puckered pink lips stretched wide over Keith's dick as he watched himself slide in and out of that perfect suction. That did it: his toes curled as he pumped his load on the wall. He slowly recovered as the water washed his lust down the drain.

He decided to grab Dominic before heading down to the meeting. *You should let his partner take him*, his subconscious warned. *There is no reason to spend so much time with or cozying up to the new guy*. But then there was just something about the man that made Keith want to get to know him better.

Yeah, that something would be you thinking with your dick.

Keith couldn't help but smirk at his own inner monologue. Stuffing his feet in his shoes and grabbing his gear, he headed out to get the man in question.

Three quick steps and he was knocking on Dominic's door. "Just a sec," was the muffled reply from the other side. Keith was right in the middle of telling himself that he could handle this infatuation when the door was pulled open.

Sweet... Fucking... Jesus. Keith had made a huge mistake.

Dominic had come to the door wearing nothing but a scrap of cloth that someone had obviously misnamed a towel. It was more appropriately named *obscene*. Keith's eyes made quick work of traveling the well-defined chest, spotting and following a lucky drop of water cutting a path to Dominic's groin.

It was a path Keith wanted to follow with his tongue.

Dominic's voice forced his attention back to the man's face. "Oh, hey, Keith, come in. I was just getting ready."

Unable to speak, Keith just gave him a wide berth once enough blood had reached his head to allow his feet to move.

Dominic

"Oh, hey, Keith, come in. I was just getting ready," Dominic said as he stepped aside to let him in. When Keith didn't move, Dominic made eye contact and saw a flicker of emotion, but it was gone before he could register what it was.

Dominic only remembered his current attire—or lack thereof—as Keith stepped widely around him, avoiding all physical contact. He'd jumped from the shower when he heard the knock at his door, afraid he was somehow late. He had rushed out of the bathroom with nothing but a flimsy towel that barely kept him decent.

He flushed; most people were taken aback when they saw his intricate bodysuit tattoo, and Keith seemed to be no exception. "Give me a sec," Dominic said as he turned abruptly to hide his quickly-growing problem from the man's steady gaze. He snatched his clothes off the bed as he strode quickly to the bathroom.

Come on, man, pull your shit together; we are not some horny sixteen-year-old. We've spent years living with men, his Angel chastised.

Dominic scrubbed his hands down his face. It was unacceptable for him to have this little control with someone he barely knew. He took his time pulling on his clothes; in his rush to hide in the fucking bathroom, he had forgotten to grab his underwear.

Looks like we're free-balling today, his Angel joked. It was hard to believe that he had managed to both behave inappropriately and embarrass himself every time he was in the same room with Keith. It was like reliving all the horrors of puberty in one day.

Once dressed, Dominic couldn't think of one logical reason why he'd still be in the bathroom, other than hiding. He glanced one last time in the mirror—he should've taken the time to shave—before heading back out into the fray.

Hopefully he could get through tonight's mission and back without acting like a total ass. So far, his past experiences said that might be too much to hope for.

Keith

Fuck. Fuck. Fuck!

Keith was ill-prepared for the slam of lust that struck him stupid when Dominic opened the door practically naked. Nothing he came across in the man's profile had suggested the breathtaking design that started just after his wrist to just before the knees. Even his long-sleeve compression shirt and shorts had hidden this surprise. Keith wondered if the tattoo covered his groin as well, but the towel obscured his view.

He had wanted to peel that towel off with his teeth and follow that sexy-as-fuck tattoo with his mouth. His cock had shot to rock-hard status so quickly that he had actually felt lightheaded. Every perverted thought he'd had about what was hidden when he'd first seen him in that tight full body compression suit and shorts paled in comparison to the glorious reality of his flesh.

Now with that blush sweeping up from Dominic's neck, Keith had to bite his cheeks hard to remain silent. He groaned internally. God, the man was beyond fuckable and pushed every button Keith possessed. He wanted to spend hours worshipping every last inch of him. Hell, Dominic made a few new buttons that were all his own.

Dammit. Trying to find a way to reverse the uncomfortable course they'd taken, Keith decided he would shoot for small talk, "I figured I'd grab you before I headed down to the briefing since you don't have your ID chip yet."

When Dominic immediately responded, "Thanks, man. I was going to knock on your door before I headed out," Keith was relieved.

Don't shit where you make your bread. It was a motto that had served Keith well since joining the team. Mixing business with pleasure could get messy, and when the person he was fucking could literally hold his life in their hands, it was a good policy to not piss them off. But looking at Dominic right now had a different head vying to make the decision for him.

This could prove to be a disaster.

Dominic

Dominic hoped the panic and relief he felt weren't noticeable in his voice. Looking at his reflection in the mirror, Dominic wondered how he was going to work with this man every day without showing his hand.

Dominic took his first deep breath when Keith started calmly chatting as if the awkward moment hadn't just happened. Thank fuck for that; he couldn't think of a thing to say to break the tension as he'd dressed, hiding in the bathroom.

When Dominic stepped back in the room, Keith was already standing by the door. They walked down to the briefing room in relative silence; apparently neither man could think of a single thing to say.

Dominic noticed that everyone else was already seated around a conference table surrounded by monitors by the time they entered the room. Natasha stopped him as soon as he entered the room and handed him a laptop, a sealed envelope, an earpiece and small transmitter/receiver, and a new cell phone.

Taking the only available seat, which just so happened to be right next to Keith, Dominic's pulse sped at their proximity. Thankfully, Keith's attention was drawn to the monitors that had the video feed from the club they were heading to, along with the faces of two men.

Lucky cleared his throat, and everyone fell into silence at his unofficial start of the briefing. The room quieted as the monitors came to life. They were targeting Russian smugglers at a well-known mob-run bar. Dominic took in his surroundings, the team members he had met earlier, and the dozen or more analysts around the room.

His suspicions that Natasha was in charge were confirmed. She was obviously second, and the way she watched him left no doubt that Dominic would be on her radar. These were bad men that needed to be taken out, but this was more of a test of his skills than anything else.

No worries, buddy. Just don't fuck this up. No pressure, his Angel dismissed easily.

Yeah, no pressure. Just run an op with people he'd just met in an area he hadn't prepped. What could be so hard about that?

Lucky

"There has been a slight change in plans regarding the number of targets and where the snipers will set up shop. Our primary kill target, Alec Ivanovo, will be meeting with a high value target of interest, Mr. Ivan Maksimov. The CIA has had this man on their radar for almost a decade. This is the first time he has ventured into the U.S., and we have been selected to make his stay here permanent," Lucky said. Photos of the target and locations flashed on the monitors, along with detailed drawings of the club's outside layout and surrounding area.

They had been tracking these smugglers for months, ever since a shipping container filled with young children had been intercepted by a random cargo search. There was little doubt that these kids had been headed for the sex trade, and it was pure luck that had saved them from that fate.

"Dominic, Steven, you two will be setting up your workshop on the roof of The Cathedral. Keith, Natasha, you will be their entry team opening the side door so they can go up undetected. You two will also be their cover during and after the sweep. There will be guards crawling all over so you will need to be their eyes and ears till they reach the roof."

The last part was directed mostly to Natasha. As his second-in-command, Lucky depended on her to keep the snipers safe in the field. She had more than earned her reputation as a resourceful field agent. He didn't need to know her history to recognize many of her skills were not the things an agent learned at the farm.

"Steven, your target will be Alec. He is a kill target. Dominic, you'll take out the guards once Steven has dropped Alec. Your primary target is Ivan. He needs to be deeply sedated, so double tap him," Lucky said, handing Dominic and Steven photos of their targets.

While this mission was mainly being used to gauge the new guy, these targets were highly valuable, so he had set up a backup sniper in case Wonder Boy here missed the mark. Though looking at his records, Lucky was pretty sure he'd found the right man to round out his team.

"Sam, you and Eric will collect Ivan. I will provide your cover. Any questions, gents?" After a few minutes of questions and side conversations, Lucky continued, "Dominic, you need to see Eric and Natasha immediately.

We will be rolling at twenty-three hundred; that means have your asses in the garage at twenty-two thirty. Dismissed."

Dominic

Dominic grabbed his intel and scanned the room for his partner, wanting to go over what signals they would use during the hunt. He'd been on plenty of missions, but he'd never gone into the field with a spotter he had never even fired on the range with. He had just made eye contact with Steven when Natasha grabbed his arm.

"You need to come with me and Eric," Natasha ordered.

She didn't even bother to wait for his response as she and Eric made their way towards the back office area. Grumbling, Dominic damn near had to scramble to keep pace with the quickly disappearing figures.

As he followed, Dominic soon realized that this was a fully-functioning infirmary with one room marked as surgery. They passed several people who seemed to be nurses of some sort before they entered an exam room that could have doubled as a doctor's office.

"Take off your shirt and lie down," Eric commanded as he started laying several syringes out. "You remember the implant you received at the training facility?"

He paused briefly.

After Dominic's affirmative nod, he continued, "That was your tracking chip. It also works as a distress signal if you press and hold it."

Eric prepped his tools, apparently not expecting or waiting for an answer.

"That," Eric supplied almost absently while pointing to Dominic's chest, "is how we found you this morning. Shock is now scrambling your signal so only she can track it."

Eric grabbed the largest syringe on the table.

"This is your RFID chip. This will grant you access to all the areas here at the Hive as well as the armory and range." He quickly implanted the small capsule then jabbed Dominic with a second needle in the shoulder, mumbling something about antibiotics. The whole process took only a few seconds; the doctor worked quickly, not giving Dominic a chance to react to the procedure.

Natasha was next up, placing some sort of device over the implant in his thumb then scanning his chest with a handheld reader.

"All right, you're online. Get dressed. The laptop and cell phone I gave you can only be accessed by you via your RFID chip. Any attempt to unlock it without you pressing your thumb to the screen will cause all data to be erased, and a tracking program will start. In the envelope, you will find your new ID, passport, birth certificate, and banking information." Natasha's mannerisms and tone were professional and short as she pointed at each of the items she had given him.

By twenty-two hundred, Dominic was in the armory signing out his M40A5 sniper rifle, one red magazine filled with knockout darts, and two clips of live rounds.

"You know how effective those darts are, don't you?" Steven drawled as he too signed out his rifles and sidearms.

Dominic couldn't smother the bitter laugh as he remembered how *effective* those darts were at putting him down during his pre-dawn jog. Hell, he had slept from Washington to just a few miles away from the Hive.

"So did you have the honor of darting me that morning?" Dominic asked as he strapped his twin Sigs in their holster.

"Nope, that was Keith. He has always been a proficient sniper." Steven laughed as he headed out towards the garage.

Well, fuck me sideways. We'll have to remember to thank Keith for that treat, Dominic's ever-present Angel noted.

Making his way to the garage, Dominic narrowed his focus to the task at hand. There was nothing like the hunt to shut out every distraction; just the target, nothing else existed. This was what he loved about his job. When he was in the zone, his fucked-up life didn't matter. With his rifle, he was the master of the universe, and it was the only time that he felt completely in control.

The trip to New York City was quick and uneventful. As they got approximately three blocks from their destination, they separated. Natasha and Keith broke off and strolled around the corner holding hands, while Dominic and Steven crossed the street.

Dominic couldn't explain the uncomfortable feeling he got as he watched Keith pull Natasha closer to his body before they disappeared out of sight. Dominic groaned; he needed to keep his head in the game, and he shook off the thought as he and Steven continued on their path. Once they came within half a block of the club, Stephen pulled out a device that looked like a tablet, but Dominic knew better.

"This is a Shock specialty. She makes the best gadgets. This baby will shut off the cameras in the back and put the feed on a loop. It also disables the alarm and unlocks the back door and roof." Steven smiled like a giant five-year-old with a brand new video game as he pressed a series of buttons.

Two minutes later, each of their earpieces came to life. "Sweeper One, this is Hive. Over." The command center analyst had a direct link into their comms. They would monitor events in real time and make any necessary changes on the fly.

"Hive, this is Sweeper One," replied Lucky as they all waited in their ready positions.

"All systems go. Verified electronic disturbance, proceed with due diligence. How copy?" asked the voice of the command center with the Hive's order for Lucky to move forward.

"Solid copy," Lucky replied.

Switching over to the mission frequency, Lucky addressed his team. "Gentlemen, let us pave the road to peace with a sweeping wave of violence." That was their cue to move.

"Well that was poetic," Dominic joked.

Steven chuckled as they made their way to their location across from the club. "Yeah, he does love his motto speeches."

Keith

Natasha and Keith stood in line to enter the nightclub. He always hated being an escort; it meant he had to go in unarmed and wait for his weapons. Not that he had any doubt that he and Shock could take out at least two dozen men barehanded, but he preferred having his piece. He wrapped his arms around Shock and leaned in as if kissing her ear.

"So, honey, are you ready to do some damage?" Keith purred. To any onlooker, they would just look like lovers embracing.

Across the street, he could see where Dominic and Steven set up at the pizza shop. The crowd around them was filled with kids that barely looked old enough to get in a club, but he doubted they did much ID checking.

Natasha giggled. "I'm always ready, baby boy. Can you keep up?" She spoke just loud enough that others could surely hear the sexual overtones. They reached the front of the line, handing the bouncer their IDs and their sixty-dollar cover charge.

What a fucking rip off.

After a thorough pat down and scan for weapons, they were both allowed inside. They would mingle for five minutes before finding their way to the side entrance separately. Each moment was timed, all the players moving in sync.

Inside the place was a cesspool of half-naked little girls. Keith got Natasha's attention and pointed out the girl dancing in a cage above the bar. He was willing to bet his left nut that the girl hadn't reached sixteen. Natasha gave him a nod of acknowledgement before making her way to the back to get Steven in.

Keith went to the bar and ordered a scotch on the rocks. On his way over, he linked up his comm to let Lucky know he was in position, and waited.

Dominic

As they sat at the pizza parlor across from the side entrance, Dominic tried to ignore the easy banter between Keith and Natasha. They were obviously comfortable with one another; Dominic couldn't help but wonder if they were partners in every sense of the word.

"Boomer," Natasha's voice came over the earpiece.

Steven got up with the duffle bag containing both rifles and ammo and headed to the door. Dominic silently watched as he entered the building, going through his objectives and steeling his nerves as he waited for his call. Four minutes later, Natasha verified his partner's position.

"Boomer reached the workshop. All clear." This meant Natasha and Steven had cleared the hallway and she was headed to the bar while Keith headed to the door.

Time to go to work.

The schedule called for a five-minute survey in between movements, ensuring that they were not being followed or watched and drawing as little attention as possible. After what seemed like hours, Keith's deep tenor beckoned, "Chaos…"

Standing up and placing the food they hadn't touched in the trash, Dominic slowly strolled across the street to the door. He took in the scene as he headed directly to the building; getting inside should be the easy part. But he had long since learned that the easy part was where a lot of people got killed.

He grabbed for the door handle and stepped inside. Keith was looking out toward the dance floor, partially hidden in the shadows. Dominic kept moving and stepped completely past Keith. Once the door closed, Keith secured Dominic's six and they moved toward the roof.

"Here," Dominic whispered as he handed Keith both his and Natasha's weapons and spare magazines.

Keith slid both weapons in the small of his back and pocketed the magazines. They froze as they heard footsteps and voices headed their way toward the stairs. Dominic looked up into a corner mirror; he could just make out three men heading for their position. Dominic swore and looked back at the spook. They locked eyes just before their earpieces came to life.

"Switch, you have three coming your way." Natasha's voice confirmed what Dominic already knew.

They were about to be spotted. As his mind raced with possible solutions of how to kill them and dispose of the bodies quickly and quietly, he was surprised when Keith threw him up against the wall.

Just before Keith smashed their mouths together, Dominic heard him mumble, "Just go with it."

Instinctively, Dominic went to push Keith away, but years of training stilled him when he heard the voices come closer. Dominic wrapped his arms around Keith, trying to discreetly place his hand on the gun Keith had tucked into his waist. Keith growled in response and pressed his larger body closer, pinning Dominic to the wall.

Dominic locked up tight; even his smartass Angel was silent. All the times he'd fantasized about what it might be like being dominated by a man paled in the face of this one moment. His heart rate doubled as Keith changed his angle, pressing his lips against him firmly and forcing him to respond.

Keith licked the seam of his mouth, demanding entry. When Dominic failed to obey, Keith slid his hand into Dominic's hair and tugged hard. Dominic's pulse skyrocketed at the rough handling, adrenaline leaving him lightheaded as blood raced to his cock. Dominic's lips parted in surprise, and Keith leaped on the gesture, shoving his tongue inside.

A low moan escaped Dominic's throat as Keith took control of the kiss, his body responding to the man as if it had no choice, all his control sucked from his soul. He felt a confident brush of tongue against his, luring him to chase it as it retreated. Suddenly, he couldn't get enough; their mouths met and tongues twined, and everything about this kiss told Dominic that this moment would forever change the course of his life.

Dominic lost track of everything except the pounding in his ears. Nothing had ever felt this good or this right, all from just a kiss. When Keith tugged harder on his hair, Dominic gasped and changed his angle, allowing Keith's tongue to delve deeper into his mouth. He shuddered and whimpered when Keith pressed closer; no doubt he could feel Dominic's growing erection pressed firmly against his hip.

As if the sound was a starter's pistol at a race, Keith shoved his thigh between Dominic's legs, causing his cock to twitch against the sudden pressure. His arousal quadrupled with the firm thigh pressing up against his aching balls.

Just as he was about to grind his cock against the equally hard one pressed against him, a disgust-filled voice pulled him into the present. "Fucking fags." Dominic cracked open his eyes to peer at the men who had caused his current predicament.

"Shut it, Bruce. Alec will have your balls for fucking with the customers." The other guy jerked his buddy's arm to get him moving again.

Keith and Dominic stayed pressed together until the elevator door opened and closed. Keith slowly pulled away, and Dominic instantly felt hollowed, gutted. He pulled himself completely into the here and now as they slowly made their way over to the steps.

He could see Natasha had placed herself in a position where she could watch the scene unfold and render assistance if they needed it. But that also meant she had seen the whole scenario. Dominic couldn't allow himself to think of this now. He needed to focus.

As they climbed the stairs, Keith watching his six, Dominic took the opportunity to pinch the underside of his

cock—hard. His erection sagged slightly; he was not going
to face his new partner with a boner.

When they reached the roof access, Keith finally
spoke. "Are you okay?"

Dominic couldn't look at him. He just bit out, "I'm
fine, we're good." Luckily Keith decided to leave it alone.
He glanced back as Keith turned to leave. "Thanks," he
said, feeling the flush on his cheeks. Keith watched him for
a moment then nodded before heading back down the
stairs.

Dominic

Taking up his position, Dominic took a deep breath to clear his head. "So, it seems you were able to avoid detection without killing the suspects?" Steven whispered from his spot right beside Dominic.

"Yeah," was his only reply. He couldn't really go into detail of how they had managed it.

Could he?

But he couldn't stop flashes of Keith's face from dancing in his mind. Luckily, their earpieces hadn't picked up the sounds Dominic had made as Keith took him apart. Steven sat patiently, as if he knew Dominic was wrestling with it or in case he wanted to elaborate.

Dominic looked at his partner. Something about the man made him feel more comfortable than he had ever felt around another soul. His gut told him he could trust Steven; even his snarky guardian Angel seemed to think this man would be an ally.

Most people would think he was crazy if he told them about the sarcastic voice in his head. But over the years, his gut had never steered him wrong. It had proved to be the difference between life and death on numerous occasions.

No reason to stop listening now.

Maybe if he had someone to talk this through with, he could make sense of his feelings. He had lied to every person he'd ever known. No one ever really got to see him. He wanted his new life to be different; he wanted to actually live it this time. Decision made, this test right here would show him how the rest of his stay in the team would play out.

Looking directly into his partner's eyes, Dominic spoke the words he had never uttered to another living soul, "Boomer, I'm gay." Confusion flashed across Steven's face, and Dominic braced for whatever fallout that might come from his confession.

"Okay… but what the fuck does that have to do with escaping detection?" he asked, completely unfazed by Dominic's big reveal.

Of all the possible responses that had run through his head, none of them had resembled the nonchalance he received.

A bubble of laughter threatened to erupt as he tried to explain. "Nothing. Well, that's not true. Switch kissed me to throw the guys off our tail. And while I know he only did it as cover, I just… I just wanted to be honest for once." By the time he finished his spiel, he had sobered; a huge knot unfurled in his chest.

"Shit, Chaos, one thing I can tell you about this group is that no one will give a fuck about who you're fucking. We're a family, but you will see that for yourself. Don't worry, I won't out you to the Hive," Steven said with a wink.

Seconds later, both their earpieces came to life. "Targets headed to kill zone. Visual." Lucky's voice drew both men back into their work mindset.

"Copy, Lucky. Targets confirmed ready on your mark," Dominic radioed as he got a lead on his target, letting his rifle aim slightly ahead to place both shots at center mass. They would reach the kill box exactly six hundred meters out, well within his comfortable firing range.

"We are in position; fire at will," Lucky acknowledged.

Within seconds of receiving the command, Steven dropped his target with a head shot. Not waiting for his prey to spook, Dominic squeezed his trigger before the first man's body hit the ground. Taking out the guards in rapid succession, he dropped his magazine in exchange for the darts.

His target had started to run, but that only made the chase that much better. Leading him by a few extra feet, Dominic squeezed the trigger, delivering the fast acting knockout dart. Eric was on the move before the target hit the ground, but Dominic couldn't worry about the pickup. He had to ensure the threats were taken care of. Quickly dumping his magazine and re-sighting for the now-prone targets, Dominic fired a second round into the guards right as Steven did.

Lucky was up and moving to provide Eric cover as soon as their cargo dropped to the ground. The quicker they retrieved their target of interest, the sooner they would be off the scene. Dominic's second shot hit its mark with ease.

Most Americans lived their entire lives happily believing that the government did not engage in assassinations on American soil, but since Dominic no longer officially worked for the government, it was a truth in semantics and they worked tirelessly to keep that veil up.

Five minutes after the first shot, their human cargo was being loaded in the van, secured for transport. Lucky proceeded to unload his shotgun into Alec and the guard's faces and bodies, rendering immediate identification and subsequent autopsy completely useless.

The ride back to the Hive was surprisingly quiet. After dropping off the target at the pre-designated area, there was nothing left to do but drive back home. The CIA would no doubt whisk him away to some unknown location for interrogation, but this team's piece of the puzzle was complete.

Sam was driving with Natasha riding shotgun, and they broke the quiet with mindless banter about some local race track.

Somehow—because the fates seemed to take pleasure in his discomfort—Dominic had ended up in the backseat with Keith.

Even with his eyes closed, he could feel Keith's gaze. He wanted to talk to him about that kiss, but there was no way he was broaching that subject with several other team members in tow.

That kiss replayed itself on a continuous loop, which kept his dick in a constant state of alert; it took all his effort to maintain just a semi with the scent of Keith's cologne wafting around him as a seedy reminder of tonight's events. He just needed to get through this ride and debriefing. After that, he would be free to return to his room and jerk off in peace.

Or you could go to Keith's room and see if he'd be willing to take the edge off for you, his snide Angel suggested.

Not fucking likely. There was no way he would risk misreading the other man's intentions, and there was absolutely no reason to believe that kiss was anything other than a distraction. He was pretty certain that Keith and Natasha were closer than just friends.

Except now that kiss was distracting the hell out of Dominic, and he had no idea how to get those thoughts out of his head.

Chapter 4

Natasha had just hung up the phone when Keith
came charging into her room. She had a good idea what this
was about, and if she hadn't already had plans for the
evening, she would draw out the torture about his little
crush. But as it was, she really needed a distraction and he
was due in just a few minutes.

"Just come on in, make yourself right at home," she
drawled. Obviously unfazed by her less-than-warm
welcome, Keith sat down at her vanity.

He seemed uncommonly nervous as he toyed with
her brushes. She would have to question why he was so
strung out about the new guy, but that would have to
happen later. Now she just needed him to say or ask what
he came for and leave.

"Hey," Keith offered hesitantly. Natasha waited a
beat, but when he failed to continue, she fell back on her
usual gruff mannerisms.

"As much as I enjoy watching you squirm, there
must be a good reason that you dragged yourself over to
my lair so soon after a mission. Shouldn't you be

meditating, or praying, or whatever you do to clear your conscience?"

"You are always so sweet to me, Natasha. And you know we can't all be soulless killing machines. You'd have to find another niche," Keith said.

Natasha checked the time. Her visitor would be here in the next thirty minutes, and she really needed Keith gone before he arrived. It wasn't like she was trying to hide anything, but she definitely did not need her baby brother lecturing her, once again, about her choice of bed partners.

"If you wanted sweet talks, you never would have come to my room. But seriously, just say what you came to say. I have to finish up a few things."

"I just wanted to ask you to do me a favor," Keith admitted, and Natasha realized where this impromptu meeting was headed. Never one to show her cards, Natasha decided to make him ask for it.

"And that would be...?" she lead.

Keith rolled his eyes before grumbling, "What happened tonight, with Dominic and me? Can you just not say anything? He's new, and I'd rather not have him tortured right out of the gate."

Even though she had pretty much guessed that this was what Keith wanted, and she had no plans to refuse him, Natasha simply couldn't resist the opportunity to tease him a little.

"Aww, isn't that sweet. What is it? You have a crush on the newbie? Don't want anyone scaring him off?"

His reaction was expected. "See that? That right there is exactly the shit I don't want you to do," Keith growled, jumping to his feet.

If Natasha hadn't had plans for the night, she would have kept at him until he freaked, but as things were, she had a pressing matter to attend to.

"Relax. If you get any more sensitive, you're gonna grow tits. I'm not going to fuck with little Dominic, okay?" Natasha brushed him off with a smirk.

Keith laughed brightly as he walked over to her by the bed, but Natasha flinched away, ruthlessly shoving away his arm as he tried to hug her. Normally she loved his affections, the only real ones since the death of her sister, but when she was keyed up after a mission, she often found it hard to accept gentle touches.

Fight or fuck: that was her natural drive during stress, and neither option was one she would ever pursue with Keith. So she needed him to leave so she could pursue her favorite outlet. Since this would be her last ride, she had every intention of making it count.

"Thank you. Now, was that so hard?" Keith smiled, unfazed by her brusque dismissal.

She focused on the vanity. "That was more difficult than you could possibly imagine."

Laughing, Keith finally headed for the door. She would only have about five minutes to prepare for her visitor, but that was enough; there wasn't a need to do anything special for him. Keith stopped short with the door just opened and turned around. She was just about to tell him to get lost when he spoke.

"Tell *Samuel* I said goodnight," Keith threw the words over his shoulder as he disappeared from the room.

Natasha laughed and headed straight to the bathroom. She should have known that she wasn't hiding anything from the man; he was always just a little too perceptive. He hadn't been gone five minutes when she heard her door again open and close, signaling Sam's arrival.

Dominic

Over the next few weeks, Dominic fought a constant battle to remain focused on the job at hand instead of that brief encounter in the hall. After that first mission, he and Steven had become a cohesive unit. More than that, Dominic considered him the closest friend he'd had since childhood; they spent hours training and getting to know one another.

Steven had told him stories about growing up on a farm and his tight-knit family. Dominic couldn't imagine what it was like with that many siblings or being raised on a farm. Being an only child, it had been just him and his parents. Neither of them had had much in the way of family and they hadn't bothered to stay in contact with what little they did have.

Steven's mom had married a black man when Steven was nine and, being in a backwoods town, Steven had had to fight his share of battles. But rather than alienate them from one another, it had helped bond the men. Steven considered the man his real father, and to this day, they maintained that bond. Dominic couldn't help the pangs of jealousy, his father hadn't shed a tear when Dominic

Ackerman died, and although it shouldn't have, that little fact hurt.

But his home hadn't been all bad. His mother had always encouraged him to do well in school, but she had never tried to get to know her son on a personal level.

Steven was quickly proving that he was someone that Dominic could trust. Trusting someone with his life always had the ability to forge an unbreakable bond, although opening up to Steven felt like more than just connecting with a partner. Dominic was creating a new family, brothers by choice: a bond stronger than blood.

The constant training and two successful missions had not been enough to distract Dominic from thinking about Keith. Or more accurately, that kiss. He knew that the kiss had just been a means to an end, a way to allow them to go unnoticed by the enemy, but that didn't explain the way he felt.

Keith himself did little to help his confusion. Not once in the weeks since had he said a word about what happened.

Did it mean anything to him? Was he even gay?

There was no way of asking him without showing his own hand. Dominic knew he was way out of his depth, having practically no experience with men—except some close encounters and anonymous back-room blow jobs— and he had no way of deciphering whether or not Keith was interested in him.

He had asked Steven about him, but his partner had simply said, "Hey, you have to talk to him. That is his story to tell." The fact that his partner would not betray a team member's confidence made him certain his trust in Steven was well-founded. But it still pissed him off that he refused to tell Dominic even the barest of details.

In one way, Dominic was sick of hiding, tired of pretending to hit on women then making up excuses to bail. But what was the alternative? Growing up strictly Catholic, his family would have disowned him if he strayed.

Didn't you do that anyway? his Angel sneered.

Although his father never spoke a word of what he suspected, their relationship had been fractured from that moment forward. Once he was in the Marines, being gay was even less of an option if he wanted to continue to be a sniper, *but so was being diagnosed with PTSD.* After leaving the service, he'd found himself in a place that seemed more stereotypical hetero.

His ever-supportive Angel added, *Hell, man, Shock is more alpha male than the average man on the street.*

Yeah, but Steven had taken the news without even blinking, Dominic answered. In fact, since that night they had grown as close as brothers. So all that was still yet to be seen was if the rest of the team would be as accepting.

Dominic sat alone in the kitchen, trying to decide how and when to come out to his teammates. It isn't like being gay came with a procedural manual.

How to come out of the closet without losing friends and family or getting your ass kicked. Sounds useful maybe we should write it, his Angel suggested.

He wanted to ask Steven his opinion, but when Dominic had stopped by his room, he was already gone. Finishing his breakfast, he decided to work through his frustration at the gym.

Sam spotted Dominic as he walked into the training area. "Hey, Dom, you're just in time. We're just having a friendly sparring match. You interested?"

"Um, no. Don't call me Dom," Dominic corrected before asking "Who's fighting?"

"Whatever you say, buddy. Natasha is taking on all challengers to defend her title. You in?" Sledge smirked.

Dominic had little doubt that Natasha would be a serious threat in the ring. Hell, on their last mission, he had watched in complete awe as she had quickly taken out three enemy combatants. He had almost forgotten to take his shot as he'd sat watching. She'd gone from smiling at her marks to slitting one guy's throat and crushing the other guy's knee with a vicious sidekick in a blink.

"Yeah, sure. I'm in. It's been awhile since I've gotten my ass kicked. But I'm sure she'll remedy that for me," Dominic joked as he went over to let Eric tape his hands.

"You know, that might not be far from the truth," Eric deadpanned as he left the ring and took his seat.

Dominic

Natasha was already in the ring with one of the members of Hive Sweeper Team Three, call sign: Viper, or something. Judging by his slow reactions, though, his moniker could have been Sloth for how effective as he was at even coming close to hitting his mark.

After toying with the bigger man, Natasha seemed to lose her shit when he managed to catch her with a backhand that split her lip. She countered by driving her elbow into his throat before her knee made contact with his diaphragm. Catching him with a flying arm bar, he was tapping out as soon as he hit the ground.

"Goddammit! I hope she didn't fracture his larynx," Eric grumbled as he jogged up to the mats.

"Come on, Doc, you know I never aim to injure them." Natasha smirked as they watched the man on the ground whine pitifully. She looked at Dominic as a slow smile spread across her face. "My title is secured, unless… You up for it, pretty boy?" she taunted.

"Are you flirting with me?" Dominic quipped.

"Well, that depends on if it's working for you or not."

He had quickly learned that Natasha had a quick wit and a sharp tongue, never hesitating to take a jab and knowing she could more than back it up. But for some reason she seemed to hold him at arm's length. At times he felt her watching him, sizing him up, but he couldn't parse out why.

He knew she was fucking with him, but he couldn't help but remember that she was the sole witness to what went down in that hallway. The fact that she hadn't said a word to anyone had to mean something. He just didn't know what. As he headed to the mat, he noticed Keith walk in, which was just the kind of distraction he did not need.

Once they made eye contact, Keith stopped and just looked at him, staring into his eyes. Dominic had no idea what he saw, but Keith finally gave a small smile before heading over towards the heavy weights.

"Hey, pretty boy. You ready?" Natasha sneered, and Dominic mentally rolled his eyes before looking back over at her.

Whatever problems they had were comprised of biting comments veiled in jest. He had no idea what he'd done to get her panties in a twist, but as Lucky's second-in-command, Natasha had the means to make his life very difficult.

"You going to keep calling me pretty boy?" Dominic climbed into the ring. Natasha smiled and nodded, opening with some light jabs that he easily avoided. He made sure to stay out of arm's length.

"Well maybe not so pretty after this," Natasha said, following up her words with an impressive roadhouse to his jaw.

And that was when shit got real.

Keith

The first thing he had noticed when he walked in the gym was Eric tending to Natasha's latest victim. Keith then made eye contact with Natasha, watching as a slow smile spread across her face as she started to speak to someone just out of sight.

Then Sam stepped away to collect the bets. To his horror he realized that her new target was Dominic. And he was walking towards the mat, already taped up for the match.

What… The… Actual… Fuck?

He had spoken to Natasha at length about his growing attraction—bordering on stalking—for Dominic, and she had expressed her take on the situation clearly. But he was still surprised, and mildly horrified, that she seemed to have set out to prove that Dominic was less than desirable.

Keith's steps faltered as his brain scrambled, trying to devise a way to extract Dominic from the ring without causing a scene. He started walking towards the mats, set on ending this before there was any blood spilt, but before he made it, Dominic turned and looked at him.

So many emotions flashed across Dominic's face in that split second that Keith couldn't decipher one before it was replaced by another. The last look plastered across his face was decidedly determination.

It seemed to Keith that Dominic felt he had something to prove, and whether he knew it or not, when it came to Natasha, he did. So against his better judgement, Keith changed direction and headed instead toward the heavy weights.

Keith went through his warm-up routine before laying into the bags. He had no idea what Dominic aimed to prove in that ring. Maybe he had noticed that Natasha was watching him for any signs of weakness.

Then again, maybe he saw this as a way to reinstate his *manhood* after that kiss. Keith hit the bags with renewed purpose.

If Dominic needed to fight to prove to himself that he wasn't gay, maybe a Shock-style ass kicking was just what he needed. Keith couldn't deny he wanted the man; the past two weeks had been hell as he'd tried to give Dominic space to come to terms with what was between them.

Keith had half expected, but mostly prayed, for him to come to his door to finish what they'd started. After the first week of awkward conversations and avoidance, though, Keith began to wonder if he just had to accept that the man might not ever be ready.

Resigned to let this play out how it would, Keith went into his normal strength-building routine, keeping a trained eye on the fight. He wasn't going to get involved, but that didn't mean he couldn't watch.

Natasha

"Hey, pretty boy. You ready?" Natasha grinned as Dominic jerked his eyes off her baby brother.

Those two were worse than school girls, pining away after each other but never having the courage to take what they wanted. She had had to threaten to break Keith's arms if he kept whining about how he didn't want to force the situation.

At first, she had warned him away from Dominic. Getting involved with a co-worker could turn real shitty, real fast, plus they knew nothing about him. After poking around his past and bugging his room, Natasha was fairly certain that Dominic was gay and that he wanted Keith, but he was also too afraid to make the first move.

Ridiculous, all of it. The sooner they fucked like tomcats, the quicker everyone could move on. They thought they were discreet, but everyone had noticed their avoidance of each other.

"You going to keep calling me pretty boy?" Dominic asked, snickering when she gave him an affirmative nod.

Natasha wanted to see how well little Dominic could fight. Too many snipers depended solely on their weapons and when faced with hand-to-hand, they were quickly neutralized. Starting off with some jabs, she was pleased to see that he not only avoided getting hit but also adjusted to the attack.

It was easy to see when he thought he knew her next move, so she warned him, "Well, maybe not so pretty after this." Natasha caught him with a wicked roundhouse to his jaw.

While Dominic had decent fighting skills, Natasha realized he would soon tire himself out with his barrage of fast jabs and blocks, all designed to minimize her ability to attack his pressure points.

After she placed a few blows to his kidneys, Natasha finally got to see what he was like when he went all out. Natasha was put on the defensive from Dominic's sudden and brutal show of force as he began to land more blows.

Capitalizing on his advantage, Dominic pressed in. In a bid to keep him back, Natasha delivered a spin kick, aiming for his throat. Dominic was able to catch her off balance as he darted left and grabbed her leg, pulling her off balance and throwing her to the ground.

Dominic made his fatal mistake by trying to force her to submit instead of going for a knockout. Most men hesitated to go for the ground and pound against a woman, and that instinct would get them killed in a real fight. *Amateurs.* Natasha smiled as he placed his arms in the perfect position for her to take control of the fight.

Smashing her head into his face twice loosened his grip enough for Natasha to grab his arm with her dominant hand. She was able to create enough space to turn and flip her body so she held him in a classic arm bar.

He would submit or she would break his arm. She applied enough pressure to assure him she was capable of following through, and he tapped after a few pulls. This had been the closest she'd come to losing in almost a year. Maybe there was something to this pretty boy after all.

Jumping to her feet, Natasha offered her hand and a smile. "Well done, pretty boy," Natasha teased as Dominic took her hand and pulled himself up off the ground.

Wiping the blood from his cut eyebrow, Dominic chuckled. Humor lit his still decidedly handsome face. "Not good enough, I suppose. Congratulations."

Eric smiled and winked at Natasha as he climbed onto the mat before schooling his features and treating Dominic's minor injuries.

"Well, this shouldn't leave much of a scar since it's in your eyebrow." Not even offering an anesthetic, Eric made quick work of the stitches over Dominic's eye. Natasha laughed as Dominic flinched each time the needle was pulled through flesh. *Pussy.*

"Look at that, still pretty after all. Word of advice, Dominic. Never give any mercy to an opponent. That will get you killed," Natasha said with a smirk as she exited the ring to hit the showers.

He was already shaking his head, dismissing her advice. Before she could rip into his ungrateful ass, Eric sent Dominic off the ring. Keith was on his way over like an eager puppy, and while she loved the man like a brother, she had no interest in watching him throw himself at the sniper. Besides, if Keith did get lucky, she'd have plenty of time to watch the cameras she had left in his and Dominic's rooms.

Once the fighting was over, everyone was quick to file out of the gym. *Sore losers.* Natasha was more interested in finding another venue to let out all the excess stress she could feel through her veins. Fight or fuck. There were only two ways Natasha knew that quieted the battle in her head. Fighting hadn't fixed it, so that just left one option.

"Hey, Dominic, those are some pretty impressive moves you have there. That's the closest anyone has come to beating Natasha in a long time," Keith said, stepping near the ring. Natasha just kept walking. It was obvious that her little brother was determined to pursue his pretty boy.

Dominic

"Hey, Dominic, those are some pretty impressive moves you have there. That's the closest anyone has come to beating Natasha in a long time," Keith said as he walked over.

Dominic's body heated as Keith's sexy voice rolled towards him. He turned in time to catch his sexy half smile but he couldn't miss the lace of humor dancing behind those hypnotically bright eyes.

"Thanks. Spent most of my down time in the Corps fighting," Dominic answered.

He attempted to keep his tone neutral and stay away from anything that might be seen as flirting. He swore that sometimes Keith was flirting with him, which did nothing to ease his confusion in this situation, but he didn't want to make it worse. Especially when Keith looked at him like he was prey, and Keith was a predator that just realized he was hungry.

Every bit of apprehension from the past few weeks dried up as he brazenly took in the man standing before him. His presence alone made Dominic's breath falter and his cock tighten with anticipation.

Yes, I definitely want this man.

That body in question was covered with a light sheen of sweat from lifting, his tanned skin shimmered under the bright gym lights. From his wide shoulders to his six pack abs, Keith's body was completely hairless.

No tattoos. Other than the small imperfection by his ear, he had no visible scars. His body was a testament of perfection, and Dominic knew he wanted to touch and taste every inch of him.

"Well?" Keith laughed. Pulled out of his visual appraisal, Dominic realized that Keith had asked him something.

Fuck, I have no idea what he said.

Yeah, that's because you couldn't quit with the eye-fucking, his Angel-turned-devil whispered.

"Say again, man? I completely missed what you said," Dominic admitted. He stammered out a shaky laugh, trying to recover from being caught staring.

Keith gave him that filthy slow smile that suggested he knew exactly what Dominic was thinking about. *Is he flirting with me?* Dominic wondered for the hundredth time.

"I said, would you mind showing me that throw you did? It was quite effective," Keith repeated. His voice had taken on a slightly husky tone that swept through him, landing squarely in his groin. Dominic had to mentally force his cock into submission before it could make its interest known.

"Sure. You want me to slow it down, or do you want to do it full speed?" He stepped back onto the mat.

"Oh, I want everything you've got, Dominic." Keith leered playfully.

Dominic bounced on his toes in an attempt to loosen his muscles. It didn't help that he had to focus on keeping his expression blank as he faced his opponent. "Your funeral," he taunted.

Keith smiled as he taped his own hands. "If you say so, champ."

"What is up with everyone and the nicknames? It's like I'm back in junior high," Dominic groaned. Since he had stepped foot in the Hive, everyone had seemed to make it their mission to call him anything and everything except Dominic. It had gotten ridiculous.

"Everyone?" Keith asked, pulling Dominic out of his head.

It took a second to understand the question before he answered, "Yeah, everyone. Sam, Natasha, you."

Keith laughed, and even though Dominic couldn't be sure, it seemed a bit forced.

"Well then. I guess I'll just stick to your name. That way I'll be special," Keith teased. Heat rose to the surface of Dominic's face as he thought of all the ways Keith could be special.

Keith

Keith gave Dominic his most devious smile as he watched heat and need flash into Dominic's eyes. Oh yes, Dominic tried to suppress it—to keep it buried—but his expressive eyes were always a dead giveaway.

Keith barely managed not to roll his own eyes at his body's eagerness under Dominic's lusty appraisal, but fuck, he wanted that man to look at him. God, he couldn't wait to get his hands on him again.

The thought of Sam flirting with him sent a flash of jealousy through him. He really had no claims on Dominic, but that fact did little to suppress the possessive urge. Needing the distraction before he said something that couldn't be explained away, he decided to get their sparring started.

Opening up with a few quick jabs to draw Dominic in, Keith quickly sidestepped Dominic's right elbow and answered with a hard open palm to his solar plexus. Before he could recover, Keith wrapped Dominic up, taking him to the ground hard.

As they wrestled for position, Keith was able to pin Dominic on his stomach as Dominic wheezed and struggled, trying to free his arms.

Every move ground Dominic's ass against Keith's crotch until he thought he might come in his pants if the man kept squirming. As he tilted his ass up, trying for some sort of leverage, Keith couldn't help but to press his cock—which had been partially hard since he walked into the gym—against Dominic; grappling shattered his control.

Dominic immediately stilled, and his pulse skyrocketed against Keith's arm. Dominic had to feel Keith's dick press against his ass and he was in no way objecting.

This seemingly heterosexual man that invaded his every unconscious—and most of his conscious—thought couldn't have been as straight as Keith had thought. There was no way he was misinterpreting the way Dominic arched back up against him.

Feeling brave, Keith whispered, "Mmm, do you like that?" into Dominic's ear. Almost without his permission, Keith's hips thrust forward, grinding his steely length into Dominic.

Dominic

He couldn't think. He couldn't speak. All his words were locked in his throat as lust burned in his groin. He must have stayed silent too long because he felt Keith's entire body tense before he made to move away.

His lust swiftly morphed into panic as he realized that his lack of agreement had been taken as rejection. He had to do something to convince Keith that the hesitation had just been his shock and not repulsion of the situation. Before he had time to question his own logic, Dominic pushed up and rolled, surprising them both when he landed on top.

"Fuck, Dominic. I'm sorry, I thought... shit. It doesn't matter what I thought," Keith stammered as he tried to push Dominic, who had straddled his hips, off of him.

Keith narrowed his eyes as Dominic pushed back hard against him, grabbing his arms to keep him pinned to the mat. "Dude... Let. Me. Go," Keith grumbled as he began to struggle in earnest. What started as embarrassment seemed to abruptly morph into agitation at being restrained.

Dominic wasn't sure what it said about him, but the more Keith fought against him, the more his dick throbbed.

He knew that he didn't want to let this opportunity pass. No, not even the threat of violence he saw flash in Keith's eyes made him want to let the man go. It was a revelation—a kink he didn't even know he had—but it was turning him the fuck on.

Dominic maintained the tight grip he had on Keith until Keith finally stopped struggling. They watched each other for a moment before Keith's eyes dropped to his lips. Figuring he had nothing to lose, Dominic let go and did what he had been dreaming about since that night in the hall of the nightclub.

He tightened his grip around Keith's wrists, knowing he would leave bruises, canted his hips, and ground his cock against Keith's as he growled, "Stop fucking fighting me."

Then without a second thought Dominic slammed his mouth over the one that had tempted him beyond sanity.

Keith

Shit. Fuck. Oh my God.

Keith let out a surprised whimper as Dominic pressed his lips firmly against him. Dominic removed one hand from his wrist, and it slid into his hair. Keith shivered as that hand tightened and tugged. Not wanting to be just a spectator in this mating, Keith jumped into the kiss, licking the seam of Dominic's lips, requesting entry.

Keith's lips moaned open when Dominic tugged his hair again, hard, sending a fresh wave of lust down his spine. Sliding his tongue in to sample a taste, Keith pushed his erection up against the bulge grinding down against him.

As their tongues twisted and dueled, Dominic changed his angle and deepened the kiss; it was perfect. It was demanding, brutal, and full of promise. As the need to breathe made its presence known, Keith licked the roof of Dominic's mouth before pulling back and nibbling his swollen bottom lip.

Keith sucked in a breath as Dominic continued to rub their cocks together. The jolt of pleasure melted his earlier agitation, dissolving it into a completely different feeling; just as consuming, just as potent, he was defenseless against Dominic's advances. Under any other condition, if someone had attempted to restrain him like this, Keith would have broken their arm.

But in this instance, he couldn't submit fast enough, although the situation had reversed itself—much to his surprise. He wanted to roll belly up and let the man fuck him right there on the mat like a dirty whore. His pulse sped up as Dominic went from simply dragging their erections together to humping him with intent.

Keith came to his senses, realizing that they could take this no further without risk of interruption—not to mention he had no intention of jizzing in his pants like some teenager. "Let's go to my room." His hiss melted to a moan as Dominic quickened his pace, grinding down hard; the need to come built with each stroke.

"Please... Dominic, we can't do this here," he begged. He never begged but he needed to get this man alone someplace with a bed immediately.

Dominic

Keith was begging for something, but Dominic couldn't make out his words over the blood pumping through his veins. Slowing his hips, Dominic blinked, trying to see past the haze of lust and need that had all but consumed all his senses.

Keith spoke again, but the pounding in his head matched the throbbing of his cock, making it difficult to think. He wanted—no, he needed—to rut against the man beneath him.

A spike of pain finally shocked him into hearing as Keith's fingers dug into his arm. "Please... Dominic, we can't do this here."

That suddenly reminded him that they were exposed, out in the open for anyone who happened by. Jesus fucking Christ, he was basically molesting his teammate in the fucking gym. That ice bucket of reality instantly doused his libido, and he jumped to his feet as if his ass was on fire.

"Dominic, come to my room," Keith repeated as he slowly pulled himself off the floor.

A flash of pink caught Dominic's eye and he groaned as he watched Keith lick his lips as if he was looking to recapture his taste. Dominic suddenly had vivid thoughts of sliding his dick past those sinfully talented lips.

Dominic dragged his hands through his hair, taking a shuddering breath. "I don't... I'm not... I've never. Fuck!" he tried, frustrated.

There was little doubt about what would happen when they took this to a bedroom. And honestly, he was beyond ready for whatever the man wanted to do. But his lack of experience made him hesitate and the words dried up in his mouth. How did he tell someone that he was an almost forty-year-old virgin?

His inner Angel snickered and Dominic cringed at the realization that he was a walking pop culture reference. He was so far into his own thoughts that he missed Keith's rigid, pissed off expression.

Keith

That stammered denial worked like a trigger, instantly killing his erection and twisting Keith's gut.

Fuck, if this man thinks I'm going to let him walk away this time...

If he thought Keith was going to accept some bullshit denial, he was horribly mistaken. No, there wouldn't be any more weeks of hiding.

Squaring his shoulders, Keith narrowed his eyes, "You don't what? You never what, Dominic?" he challenged.

Dominic must have sensed his doubts and understood the question. He answered quickly, his words so low Keith almost missed them, spoken almost like a confession, "No, I am... I'm gay. I've just never... I've never really been with a man. But I want to. I want you."

Although he stammered through most of his whispered declaration, that last part was said as Dominic looked Keith directly in the eyes. Keith immediately closed the gap between them and kissed him fiercely, silencing any more words.

He had considered many things about Dominic over the past few weeks, but him being gay and still a virgin to man-on-man action wasn't a scenario he had lingered on. He thought that Dominic might have never been the receiver; many closeted guys felt as long as they were the one doing the fucking, that made it less gay.

But no, this was a man who had accepted his sexuality; the way he looked Keith in the eyes during that confession showed that. But still, he had never acted on it. Obviously, there was a story there, and it was one Keith would hopefully learn.

Deciding that he had to get his man moving, Keith broke the kiss and whispered for the third time, "Come to my room, Dominic."

Keith watched as Dominic licked his lips again, greedily tracking the movement as he waited for an answer. Time slowed down as Dominic looked into his eyes. Keith had no idea what the guy was looking for; all he could do was hold still and hope he found it.

"Okay, let's go," Dominic finally answered, and Keith released the breath he hadn't even realized he was holding.

Dominic

Dominic spun on his heels, heading out of the gym and down towards the living area before he lost his nerve. He wanted this, badly, but he also had no idea how it was going to play out.

Who is going to fuck who?

It was an important factor; he had no idea which way he preferred, and he had nothing to compare it to. The fact that he'd never had anal intercourse with anyone, male or female, left him at a loss for what to expect.

Dominic had received his share of blow jobs along the way, but he'd never given one. And vaginal was not the same as anal. After high school, he could never stay with a female long enough for that type of sex—not that he'd really tried—but he could never fake enough interest in them that long. So it wasn't like he had a lot of experience with that either.

Being with a man for anal sex had never been an option before; he'd only had hook ups, and they'd never included exchanging names, let alone phone numbers. Until now. Not one to leave anything to his imagination, Dominic had done extensive research over his life on anal and oral sex and positions until he'd practically memorized the how-to guides.

As they reached Keith's door a thought rushed his mind. He had only ever been the receiver; he hadn't even returned the oral sex he'd received. Well, tonight he was going to end that.

"Hey, you okay?" Keith asked as they came to a halt outside his door.

"Yeah, I'm good. I was just thinking," he replied.

Keith continued to watch him as if he was weighing Dominic's conviction to follow through with this to its most logical conclusion. Swallowing the rush of nervousness at Keith's intense gaze, Dominic stepped closer, placing his hand on the small of Keith's back.

"Invite me into your room, Keith." His voice had gone so rough and husky that he barely recognized it.

Chapter 5

Keith opened the door and stepped to the side. Dominic strolled in and looked around, taking in his environment. His room was mostly like all the others, but he had taken time to make it feel more like a home. Closing and locking the door, Keith hurriedly stepped up behind Dominic, close enough to feel the other man's body heat.

"Do you mind if I take a quick shower?" Dominic asked without turning around.

Caught slightly off guard, Keith fumbled. "Um, sure… I'll just grab us some drinks while I wait. cause I already showered… at the gym."

Shut up, shut up, just shut the fuck up! Keith chastised himself.

He had no idea why he was completely fucking this up; he was tripping over himself and looking like an ass in the process. He hadn't been this nervous when he'd lost his virginity, but Dominic made him feel almost desperate in a way he just couldn't explain.

It was more than lust; he wanted this man; no, on some levels he felt as if he needed to be with Dominic. His father always told him that he had fallen in love with

Keith's mother the minute she looked at him. At first, he thought his father was just looking back at that meeting through the love he felt now. But when Dominic had looked at him that first day, Keith had known he was a goner.

"Um… okay? I'll be just a few minutes," Dominic answered, as that slight blush returned to his neck.

Keith was pleasantly surprised when Dominic stepped forward and gently kissed him. Keith was awed by the warmth that bloomed within his chest at the feeling of that soft press of lips. Dominic seemed to have shed the uncertainty that hovered around them in the gym. Keith didn't know if it was confidence or bravado, but he wanted to keep him just like this.

Keith stood there until Dominic went into the bathroom and started the shower. He practically raced from his room toward the kitchen area to grab a couple of waters and sandwiches; they would hold up in his fridge.

He was so consumed with getting what he needed and getting back to the sexy, naked man currently in his shower that he didn't notice anyone else enter the room.

Natasha teased, "So still playing that cat and mouse game? I've never thought you the type to play the role of a young boy with a schoolyard crush, Keith."

The sound of Natasha's voice not only surprised him, but even managed to wilt the erection that had persisted since the gym. He turned around and shot his best friend his best *drop fucking dead* glare as he turned back to the fridge, grabbing supplies before she could continue to grill him.

"What's the matter, Keith? Everyone can see he has a hard on for you. Why haven't you closed the deal?" Natasha teased as she continued to watch him in that almost creepy way she had.

Keith rolled his shoulders in aggravation. Natasha could get him riled up so easily lately that their teasing little games were beginning to lose their appeal.

"I thought you said dating him was a bad idea? What made you change your mind, Natasha?" He couldn't turn around or hide his annoyance from her.

"Who said anything about dating?" she asked incredulously. "I was thinking that if you fucked him through the headboard, maybe you would stop being led around by your dick."

Keith took a deep breath to both give himself some time to think and remember that Natasha was his best friend; this was her standard operating procedure. She was never one to pussyfoot around any topic, especially sex. Once he was sure he had a tight leash on his agitation, he turned to eye his friend as she flashed him a filthy grin.

"Natasha, why do you turn every encounter into one of your sordid ideas of sex and relationships?" he groaned as he realized she knew exactly what he was up to. Hell, she may have even been watching them go at it in the gym.

He didn't doubt that she had equipment she could use to monitor anyone at any time. He also didn't doubt that she wouldn't hesitate to use said equipment against him. She received way too much pleasure from making him squirm.

Keith bit the inside of his cheek, trying unsuccessfully to hide his smile as she waggled her eyebrows suggestively.

"Come on, Keith. You love my sordid ideas, not to mention my absolutely filthy sex stories. And unless you're planning on binge eating tonight, I'm going to take the double rations you're carrying as a clue that I may have spoken too soon and that you'll soon have some sordid sex stories of your own." Natasha smirked as she raised her eyebrow in question.

He felt his ears burn as a blush rose up his neck, but there was no way he would give her the satisfaction of an answer. For one, he had too much respect for the man in his room, and secondly, Dominic was no off-handed fuck buddy.

This was someone that he felt he really had a chance to have something with. And finally he had to admit, if only to himself, that he was more than halfway in love with the man he had studied religiously over the past two weeks.

Refusing to rise to her dirty bait, Keith simply shook his head as he headed back to his room. Her laughter accompanied him all the way down the hall. She cackled, "Apparently falling in love hasn't done much for your sense of humor, *mladshiy brat!*"

Returning to his room, Keith made quick work of storing the food and drinks in his fridge then made sure the door was locked and alarmed. It would be just like Natasha to pay them an uninvited visit, and with that in mind, he locked the safe room's deadbolt. There was no outside access to it.

Hearing Dominic still in the shower, Keith decided to grab his supplies and stash them in an easy-to-reach location. He wasn't going to assume they would be having anal sex, but he knew they would be having orgasms one way or another, and he didn't want to have to stop once they got started.

Keith placed the lube and condoms under his pillow; he took the gun he normally stored there and placed it in his bedside drawer. He was just about to put on some music when he heard the water shut off. Pushing play, he smiled as the sensuous and melodic tones of Placebo poured through the speakers.

"Hey, I just realized I have no clothes here," Dominic laughed nervously. The sound of his voice invited Keith to turn and damn near drool at the vision he displayed.

Wearing nothing but a flimsy towel and that intricate tattoo that covered the majority of his awe-inspiring body, Dominic was every gay man's wet dream come to life. All sense of reason and caution vanished as his interested cock jumped in his pants, demanding a lot more of the blood his brain needed to form coherent thought.

"Well that just means I won't have to undress you again," he replied, his voice gone gravel rough.

Crossing the room quickly, Keith stepped in front of Dominic and eyed the small towel that barely hid any part of his body. He watched with rapt attention as Dominic's nostrils flared and his breathing increased.

As if in slow motion, Keith reached out to place his hand on Dominic's chest, where Keith could feel Dominic's heart thundering away like a stampede of horses as the distance between them shrank.

Angling his head, Keith pressed their lips together, cautiously, feeling out his welcome since their last kiss— not wanting to rush and scare Dominic away.

Gently licking between the seam of his lips, Keith gave an appreciative sound low in his throat when Dominic immediately opened them. Keith tightened his grip to fuse their bodies together. Dominic's hands were back in his hair as their tongues dueled for dominance, and Keith was determined to make this man his.

Adjusting his angle, Keith got his entire body to move, grasping Dominic's hips firmly and maneuvering him towards the bed. Dominic gasped against his mouth when the back of his legs made contact with the mattress. Keith tugged the flimsy towel away as he gave his man a gentle push.

Dominic

Dominic lay panting on the bed as he looked up at his soon-to-be lover who was, for some reason, frustratingly still fully clothed. Before Dominic could utter a word of protest, Keith grabbed the hem of his own T-shirt, pulling it up and off then flinging the offending article across the room.

Keith paused, blatantly basking in the attention as he reached down and slowly began removing his shorts. He'd gone commando, and his erection slapped against his abs, leaving a smear of pre-cum when it was released.

"I was wondering how far that tattoo reached," Keith said as he lowered himself onto the bed, instantly making contact from knees to hips.

Dominic could only moan as he watched Keith run his hands across Dominic's hairless chest until he reached a nipple, pinching it gently. Dominic arched, the sensation forcing out a hiss as he pushed into that calloused hand.

"Fuck," Dominic groaned when Keith pinched harder, rolling that sensitive nub between his fingers. Somehow the sensation traveled directly to his cock, causing it to jerk painfully.

"Do you like that, baby?" Keith crooned in his ear.

It was weird being called baby. But when Keith ducked his head and captured his one nipple in his mouth, sucking hard as he tweaked the other, Dominic couldn't find it in him to care. His breath caught when Keith bit down hard on his nipple before he licked away the hurt, that sudden burst of pain seeming to intensify his overall pleasure.

"Do you like that, baby?" Keith asked again before giving the other nipple the same biting and licking treatment. Dominic couldn't form enough words to respond as pleasure danced around his nervous system, blocking everything but the ache in his balls.

Keith had the nerve to chuckle when Dominic could only manage whimpers and mewls in response to the onslaught, but he was too lost in the pleasure to manage words. Biting and kissing his way down Dominic's tattooed chest, Keith traced the intricate patterns as his teeth and tongue snaked their way down his chiseled torso.

He had planned to seduce Keith, and he'd spent his time in the shower coming up with a plan to take control of the situation, to take Keith apart with his hands. But now with Keith pressed against him, tormenting his skin with bites that were sure to bruise, those thoughts were ditched somewhere along with his towel.

Keith

Keith kissed his way down Dominic's torso, wanting to taste every inch of exposed flesh. The sounds Dominic made as he made his way to his nipples were obscene. Dominic shuddered as Keith's hands roamed lower to trace a fingertip up Dominic's erection. Wanting to hear more of those sounds, Keith mouthed the path his hands had.

Pausing to drag his teeth across Dominic's hip, Keith looked up to see Dominic carefully watching him through hooded eyes. Wanting to keep his attention, he gripped Dominic's cock without breaking eye contact and stroked him slowly from root to tip. Dominic choked and arched his spine as Keith used his thumb to swipe against the sensitive tip, collecting the pre-cum that had gathered there.

Keith waited until he caught Dominic's glazed eyes then smiled and winked, before he dipped his head as he swallowed the entire length. Dominic quickly bucked his hips, and Keith nearly gagged on the intrusion; he had to push Dominic's hips down firmly to pin him to the bed before relaxing his throat to take him deeper. Just once.

He pulled back until only half was in his mouth. Keith wanted to keep him on the edge, make the pleasure so intense that his body completely relaxed. But he also just wanted to be able to breathe. The man had a large dick and deep throating him would not be easy, so Keith hummed around the length in his mouth to heighten the sensation.

Dominic gasped and gripped the sheets when Keith tightened his lips and teased his tongue at the head of his cock. Keith let out a moan of his own as he took Dominic all the way, sinking down until he could feel the tickle of Dominic's neatly trimmed pubic hair.

Dominic gave up trying to fuck Keith's mouth after a few seconds but Keith wrapped a hand around the base just in case. Instead, he wove his hands through Keith's thick hair and began to use it as a leash to drag him up and down his shaft. Keith allowed him to set the pace; breathing through his nose, he focused on not gagging. Dominic's back arched higher as Keith continued to suck, his hands no longer gripping, but petting, and Keith realized Dominic must be getting close.

He wouldn't let Dominic come, not yet, but he wanted to take him right to the edge. He wanted him begging for it by the time Keith got his fingers in him.

Keith didn't worry about the drool sliding down his fingers, no doubt pooling in Dominic's crack.

It was less than a half dozen more strokes before Dominic's hips slammed up as he moaned, "Fuck. Switch, I'm close."

Keith growled around the flesh in his mouth before pulling off. "Call me Keith. I want to hear you say my name, baby," he said as he caught Dominic's blissed out expression.

Dominic

Dominic moaned, fighting desperately against the orgasm crawling up his spine. Keith immediately released him, hands and mouth gone.

Keith growled around him and Dominic felt his release well up until Keith gripped the base of his cock almost to the point of pain. Between the loss of Keith's mouth and that tight grip, his orgasm jackknifed to a stop. His balls ached at the sudden diversion. Dominic jerked up to see Keith pull back and lube three of his ridiculously large fingers.

He chose to ignore the threat of having them impale him and focused on his lack of orgasm. "Goddammit, Keith! Why'd you stop?" He could hear the whine in his own voice, but he was desperate to come and didn't give a fuck how needy he sounded.

"Relax, baby. It might hurt less if you come first," Keith said, stroking him slowly.

Dominic fell back against the sheets and murmured, "Bastard," as Keith sucked the tip of his cock back between his lips, focusing on the sensitive tip.

Pulling back from the tip, Keith switched to licking Dominic's cock from root to tip as he started to circle his virgin-tight ring of muscles. He slowly increased the pressure on each pass until the tip of one finger breached that tight barrier.

"Shit," Dominic gasped and clenched down.

Fuck. God damn... Shit.

That fucking burn tore up his spine as Keith's thick finger pushed all the way inside him. Luckily, Keith immediately stilled and went back to sucking Dominic's slightly deflated cock. Slowly, the flames in his ass were doused with pleasure, and it curled its way back from his dick up his spine.

He couldn't hold back his embarrassing little gasps and moans if his life depended on it. After a few seconds, Keith pulled back and pushed in in perfect sync with his bobbing, talented mouth. Pleasure had just started radiating from Dominic's once-virginal hole when Keith abruptly added a second finger.

Dominic let out a startled yelp as the pleasure that had been slowly building warped into a flash of fire that threatened to make him fly from the bed. Pain locked up his spine and halted his breath as Keith redoubled his effort, adding an obscene amount of pressure that immediately outweighed the intrusion.

Dominic couldn't separate the sensations coursing through his body. One half was extreme pleasure, and the other half was pure pain. They seemed to be feeding off each other, twisting, merging into a feeling that had him needing more. Keith's hand replaced his mouth, jacking Dominic's dick as those devious digits scissored him open.

Fortunately, Keith chose that moment to take the entire length of Dominic's cock back into his mouth and continued to apply pressure until the pleasure outweighed the pain. The digits inside him remained completely still until Dominic felt his tightly-clamped muscles relax and yield.

He waited until the sensation slid from burning to a dull ache before tentatively thrusting into Keith's mouth again. Apparently taking that as his cue to continue, Keith slowly fucked him with those fingers. Soon, it wasn't enough and he began to push back onto that invader. Frustratingly, Keith chose that moment to pop his mouth off of Dominic's cock.

Keith

Dominic growled and Keith had to beat back his laugh at his pissed-off expression. Keith knew his man was on edge, but timing was everything.

He didn't want Dominic to come until he was prepped. Keith wanted to be able to push inside him the second Dominic reached his first climax, when he should be relaxed enough to make that first push as painless as possible.

"That's it, baby. I know it sounds counterproductive, but I need you to push out as I push in," Keith encouraged him. "Fuck, Dominic. You're so fucking tight. I can't wait to get my dick inside you," he growled. Dominic's ass slowly relaxed as he pushed out with those stubborn muscles.

"Come on, baby. Move with me." Keith groaned as he rocked his dripping cock on the bed to try and ease the pressure.

He wanted to get his dick into Dominic's tight ass, but he couldn't risk rushing this first time. The pain of penetration couldn't be completely avoided, but he could make the pleasure so great that the pain would be easily forgotten.

Dominic must have started to feel the benefits from Keith's prepping; he began to writhe and push back with increasing speed. Keith needed to add another finger to help widen that impossibly tight passage, but he didn't want Dominic to completely lose the pleasure that he was now riding. Curling his fingers, Keith sought out that small bundle of nerves that would make this process seem well worth the discomfort.

Keith kept up the hand job, alternating between twisting his fist around the sensitive tip and sucking Dominic's balls. He had to be careful to not push him too far over; he needed Dominic to hover right at the edge.

Coming too soon could make getting fucked painful and might throw him off bottoming for the foreseeable future, which would be self-defeating. So patience was Keith's friend, even as his own cock begged and wept for attention.

After what seemed like an eternity, Dominic shouted and arched his spine then slammed himself back on

Keith's fingers, and he knew he had found what he was looking for.

Keith almost wept in relief as he gave that elusive prostate a gentle rub, curling his fingers in a come hither motion. He added more lube to both his fingers, drenching Dominic's ass in the slickness.

Dominic

Dominic eagerly spread his legs farther, moaning low in his throat. He couldn't help but wiggle and moan like the wanton slut he was quickly becoming as Keith continuously stroked that spot that made his toes curl and his eyes cross. He barely noticed the ridiculous amount of lube that now covered him from his balls to his ass, soaking the sheets.

A tinge of pain radiated from his ass as Keith added yet another finger, but the prostate massage rendered that unimportant; it almost seemed to jack up his need to come. Almost immediately, that too-full feeling was replaced by a need for more, deeper, harder—Dominic knew those fingers wouldn't bring him the pleasure he sought. Pushing back harder forced those fingers to nail his prostate, head on and hard, and it spiked his need for more to an unprecedented level.

Giving up any pretense of modesty, and releasing his embarrassment, he found himself asking, no, *begging* Keith to fuck him. "Switch! Fuck, I need—" he gasped as Keith grazed that spot. His cock throbbed each time Keith pressed in, and if Dominic had known it would feel this good, he would have shoved something up his ass years ago.

"Jesus… Fuck… Please, Switch," he begged again, only to be rewarded with Keith rubbing that spot furiously as he gripped the base of Dominic's cock, killing any hopes he had of climaxing.

"Goddammit," Keith bit out, his voice almost a growl. "Say my name, Dominic!" Keith demanded again as he switched back to just barely grazing that magic spot.

Without hesitation, Dominic moaned, "Keith! God... Please, fuck me, Keith." He would call the man anything he fucking wanted if he would just keep going. Mercifully, Keith let him fall over the edge into his orgasm so strong that his back bowed and his legs twitched.

Keith gave his prostate one more quick rub before pulling out completely. Dominic didn't know if he should rejoice in the fact that he was about to get what he so desperately needed or cry at the loss of those talented fingers, but the emptiness was overwhelming.

He tried to clench his fatigued muscles, but he felt as if his hole was gaping, a mixture of pre-cum, lube, and spit dripping down and soaking the sheets. Not even his dick seemed ready to give up. His erection flagged slightly, a flush lingering from the force of his climax. He didn't want to imagine what he must look like with his legs spread obscenely, begging like a two-dollar whore to be filled.

"It will be less painful on your hands and knees," Keith ordered, patting his hip gently. Dominic was thrilled he managed to not kick the man in the face as he scrambled to comply. He had never felt so wrung out. As the rough words reached his ears, all Dominic could even think of doing was getting into the position Keith wanted.

Keith

Keith was on edge as he tore open the condom and rolled it down his length, that slight friction almost enough to push him the rest of the way. He fought his fast-approaching climax. Keith almost shouted *thank you, God* when Dominic quickly rolled to his stomach and pushed up to his knees.

Not wanting to risk tearing any delicate tissues, he added even more lube to the condom and settled between Dominic's trembling legs. Taking his own cock in one hand, Keith used his free hand to gently rub Dominic's ass.

"Just relax and push out when I push in just like before," he soothed as he spread apart those cheeks and slid the tip of his cock to Dominic's entrance.

Dominic took a deep breath in and slowly blew it out as Keith added pressure against that soon-to-be-desecrated place. Dominic moaned as Keith slid around his rim, adding more and more pressure on each pass.

When Keith felt Dominic push out against him, he shoved forward until he slipped into the tight inferno just beyond the tip.

They both immediately stilled and cried out unintelligibly, and just as quickly, Dominic clenched down on Keith's dick.

"Fuck, babe," Keith hissed as he rubbed his hands up and down Dominic's sides, giving them both a moment to adjust to this new connection. Keith peppered as much of Dominic's face as he could reach with kisses, encouraging him to relax.

Dominic's entire frame vibrated as he fought to breathe through the pain of a much larger stretch and burn. Keith knew from his first time that no one ever anticipated how it felt to be splayed open like that.

Holding his hips flush for what felt like eons, Keith counted to a hundred and back again. "You okay? Are you ready for me to move?" he asked, even as he fought with every strain of discipline he had ever learned to remain still, to resist slamming into the tightest hole he had ever experienced. Sweat glistened on Dominic's back and Keith's mingled with it as it fell from his forehead.

"Y-y-yeah… Just… Just go slow," Dominic groaned, his voice pained as he experimentally moved his lower half.

That sound was enough to bring Keith back from the edge and renew his vow to make this good for Dominic. He wanted this to be the best fuck of Dominic's life; he wanted to leave his mark so deep that no one else would ever come close.

Keith realized that his possessiveness should scare him, but he honestly didn't care. This need had brought him to a new level of insanity, and he was determined to drag Dominic there with him.

Dominic

Dominic was eternally thankful for Keith's impressive control as he slowly pumped his hips, sinking his cock further in at a glacially slow pace. Civilizations had ceased to exist by the time he finally felt Keith's trimmed public hair pressed against his ass, and finally… finally he was in.

Jesus fuck, it's like I'm being fucked by a yard stick.

He couldn't control the pain-filled sound that followed the barely-there movements, and Keith completely stilled against him. Dominic could feel Keith's body vibrating with pent up need. Dominic's heart fluttered; he wanted to make this good for Keith as well. Keith gently rubbed his back and shoulders as he waited for him to adjust to his girth.

"Okay, how about I stay still for now? Just move against me when you're ready," Keith gritted out.

Dominic could only hope his jerky head movements he made resembled a nod. He had lost the ability to string together a coherent thought, and couldn't really trust his voice for more than pained gasps.

As the pain slowly seeped away, Dominic gave an exploratory wiggle of his hips. Keith's hand immediately left his hip to stroke Dominic's now completely flaccid cock, lubed palm slowly bringing him back to life. As the pleasure once again started to rise, Dominic gently moved to Keith's rhythm, fucking himself on Keith's cock.

"That's it, slow and easy. I'm gonna move with you. Tell me if it's too much," Keith warned.

Keith gently moved inside of him, his thrusts short and slow. As Dominic's cock was brought back to full erection, he noticed the pain was almost completely gone; his muscles relaxed with each thrust in. Keith maintained his ministrations, one hand rubbing his back, shoulders, and ass while the other tugged on Dominic's renewed erection.

"You ready?" Those two words were Dominic's only warning before Keith rubbed his thumb against Dominic's now-leaking tip and pushed in, simultaneously snapping his hips forward.

Dominic pulled his hips forward into that touch before he slammed back. Keith's cock hit his gland straight on, sparks flickering behind his eyelids as he cursed loudly.

Dominic wailed as red-hot pleasure raced up his spine, curling his toes. "Fuck! Yes! Jesus, yes!"

"Thank fuck," Keith said.

Keith

Keith felt Dominic's muscles finally relax around him. He was relieved when Dominic's pained gasps slowly melted into moans as he grew accustomed to having something larger than fingers inside him. Keith didn't want to stop, but if Dominic didn't want to go on... But now all Keith could hear were the stuttered ahs of a man enjoying a good fuck.

Dominic was taking to bottoming with enthusiasm. Some men never enjoyed being penetrated, and while Keith had no problem getting off other ways, Keith was grateful that Dominic wasn't one of them.

Keith had no issues getting fucked himself, but after sliding into Dominic, he knew he would want to be here often. Gripping Dominic's hips with both hands, Keith quickened his pace as the gorgeous man started to fuck back against him.

"Oh, God... Oh, God... Oh, God..." Dominic chanted when Keith canted his hips, forcing his cock to hit that sweet spot on every thrust.

"That's it. You're doing so good," Keith praised.

Gritting his teeth, Keith fought against his urge to slam into his man too hard, but every thrust in revved up his need to fuck and rut like an animal. Sweat streamed from his hairline and into his eyes when he pushed the long locks from his face.

"Please… I need…" Dominic cried, his back drenched in sweat as he moved counterpoint to Keith's thrust.

Dominic dropped his shoulders to the mattress, which tilted his ass up, allowing for deeper penetration. They both bit out a curse as Keith slid in to the hilt—balls deep. Each thrust threatened to undo his good intentions. Dominic was still so tight, almost too tight, and Keith just wanted to slam into him and create that friction he needed.

Keith carefully picked up the pace a little more, and judging by Dominic's reaction, he was ready for more. "Harder. Please, Keith, fuck me harder," Dominic moaned, pushing back in emphasis.

Finally given the permission he so desperately wanted, Keith let go and proceeded to fulfill his man's request to fuck him harder, unable to stop the dirty commentary that followed.

Dominic

Keith's hand had left his cock but the need to come had not lessened in the least. Dominic vaguely wondered if he could come just from Keith's cock inside of him. Dominic continued to mewl and whimper embarrassingly as he clenched against Keith's cock, signaling his impending release. But his climax stayed just outside his reach. He needed more, but he was afraid to move and risk losing the perfect rhythm Keith had set.

"Oh, God... Keith... Please... I need... I need to stroke my cock," Dominic stuttered as his balls pulled up tight and his ass began the rhythmic pulse. Dominic's entire body seemed to throb to the same rhythm, and he couldn't risk moving to take his dick in hand; he was too afraid to do anything that might change the wonderful things he felt.

"Fuck no, baby, not yet!" Keith bellowed as he slammed in hard, rougher than he ever had so far. "Dammit, Dominic. You're still so fucking tight. So wet and desperate to come," he continued. A spike of pain flared as Keith tightened his grip on his hip.

Dominic let out a gasping, choked off, and desperate cry as Keith slammed into him again and again, hitting his prostate with brutal accuracy. But Keith didn't slow down, utter filth pouring out of his mouth as his hips beat out a relentless pace.

"You like it. Don't you, baby? Tell me. You gonna spread those legs any time I want? Put this pretty little ass in the air for me?" Dominic wasn't sure if Keith really expected a verbal answer, but there was no way he was forcing out words when he could barely catch his breath.

So he spread his legs further, his spine flexing. He grunted out something incoherent into the pillows. Keith must have taken it as the acknowledgement that it was, because Dominic's spine felt like it would snap with the next thrust he delivered.

Keith's hips never stopped moving, and Dominic could only let himself get fucked within an inch of his life as Keith pulled him back into each thrust. He was given a moment of reprieve as Keith ground into him. His prostate swelled as it was nudged, nudged, and nudged again.

"Fuck, look at that," Keith moaned as he spread Dominic's cheeks wide. Dominic didn't need to turn his head to know that Keith was watching his cock move inside Dominic's gaping hole.

Dominic thought he had gone past the point of embarrassment, but he couldn't deny the burst of shame, the *dirty, filthy, wrong,* that tightened his balls at Keith's brash appraisal. Luckily Keith didn't seem able to keep up the slow fuck and he was soon back to slamming in.

Keith

The bed shook, slamming into the wall, the music drowned out by their animalistic grunts. Finally, when Keith couldn't hold out any longer, he reached down and grabbed Dominic's angry, red, and furiously leaking dick.

"Come on... come on... come for me," Keith growled. With just two strokes, Dominic spilled his load, his seed shooting hard as his cock jumped in Keith's hand.

That did it; as Dominic's ass clamped down on Keith's cock, almost painfully tight, it ripped his orgasm up and out of his balls. Keith was amazed he didn't blow the condom off.

"Are you okay, baby?" Keith asked, his voice strained as he struggled to regulate his breathing.

Keith's heart beat madly and his entire body felt wrung dry. That had been the single best fucking orgasm of his life, and if he didn't know before, he knew it now: he was truly fucking gone for this man. He was all in. A tendril of fear curled in his chest.

"Yeah... I'm good," Dominic wheezed out.

Keith shifted, his now deflated cock slipping free as he kissed Dominic's neck and shoulders before rolling beside him on the bed. They laid there in silence and Keith couldn't help but wonder what Dominic was thinking. Keith couldn't trust himself not to ask or say something else equally as needy, so way before his sex addled brain was ready he forced his wobbly legs to move.

"Stay here, babe. I'll get something to clean us up," Keith said, and he quickly pressed their lips together before he headed off to the bathroom.

Keith needed a few minutes to figure out what he was going to do with the man in his bed. Turning on the hot water, he grabbed a rag and wiped himself off before the water had a chance to warm up.

It was funny how during the chase, he had never considered what he would do once he caught Dominic. *How do I keep him?* The fact that Dominic self-identified as gay had come as a shock, but he had also seemed settled and content being buried deep inside his closet.

Keith knew that a person telling their new lover that they were gay was different than telling the world. Would he want to live openly as a couple?

Keith had to admit, at least to himself, that he was the last person that would counsel someone on relationships. He had never been able to find someone who wanted to commit. Keith sent up a quick prayer that Dominic would not be one of those guys. Grabbing a clean, warm rag and a towel, he headed back to play the part of considerate lover.

Dominic

Dominic had collapsed on the bed, unable to support his own body weight when the air had been pushed out of his lungs by his lover sprawled out on top of him. He could barely manage a moan of protest as every bit of him melted into the bed.

Wrecked. That was the only word he could think of to describe his current condition: completely and utterly wrecked. He smiled into the mattress as Keith began to massage every bit of flesh he could reach in their current position.

While he took a mental inventory of his well-used body, he smiled as he cataloged his battle scars. Although he was not surprised at the ache in his ass, or the bruises he could already see taking shape on his hips, he was a bit taken aback by his sensation of total laziness. He didn't want to move; he wasn't even sure he could. But what was truly unexpected, and more than a little frightening, was the tightness he felt in his chest.

Falling for your first fuck? Better make sure we still have our dick, his Angel accused.

Dominic closed his eyes when he heard the bathroom door close. Now what? He knew what he wanted, but had no fucking clue how to ask for it. How was this going to change things? What were they now? Lovers… fuck buddies?

After what had to be the best night of his life. Dominic didn't want to ruin it by worrying about tomorrow. He startled when a warm cloth swept across his inner thigh.

"Relax, babe. We gotta clean the lube off before it dries," Keith whispered as he continued to clean his thighs and moved between his cheeks.

"I can do that," Dominic slurred as sleep attempted to claim him. He tried to move, to clean up his own mess, when Keith stopped him.

"Don't. I know you can do it, but let me," Keith admonished as he pushed Dominic's legs further apart, seeking better access. After gently cleaning his balls, cock, abs, and ass, he threw the rag in the direction of the bathroom and climbed into bed beside him.

Dominic rolled to his side to get a better look at his bedmate when suddenly he realized he was free to ask the question that had been rattling around his head for weeks. "Where are you from?" he asked.

Keith raised an eyebrow in question but remained silent.

"Your accent. It's subtle and I can't place it," he added when it seemed Keith wasn't going to answer.

Keith

"I'm originally from Israel." Keith shifted until he was sitting up against the headboard. "My mom was an American doctor working at a hospital when she met my father. He was in the Israeli army, a spy who worked closely with the American government. They were married, and I was born two years later." Keith closed his eyes as the memories flooded him.

Figuring now was the time to tell his life's story, he decided to tell the whole tale of how he became what he'd become. It only seemed fair since he had pried into Dominic's past without his knowledge. That was something else he was going to have to share. Keith knew from experience that the more he tried to keep things a secret, the faster they were exposed.

"My mother died when I was eighteen, a terrorist bombing of a market not far from where we lived. After that, I began my training to follow in my father's footsteps."

Keith took a breath, wanting to finish the story.

"I was offered the opportunity to work for the CIA at 25; being a dual citizen put me in a unique position to aid both governments. After my father's death, I opted to stay here. There is nothing left for me in my home country."

"I'm so sorry for your loss," Dominic whispered as he gently kissed Keith's lips. "Thank you for sharing that with me," he added. Keith wrapped his arms around him as they laid curled together in a comfortable silence.

Keith took another deep breath as he cuddled closer to Dominic. Sharing his past always reminded him of all the things he'd lost. His parents had always surrounded him with unconditional love, and he had drifted aimlessly since their deaths.

But being with Dominic made him think that maybe he had a chance to create that life for himself. Even though they had made love, they had never said what this all meant, and it was time to remedy that problem.

They laid together in silence, and Keith was grateful that Dominic hadn't tried to offer any placating words. He only snuggled in closer, silently offering his comfort and consolation through touch. It didn't take long; Dominic's breathing slowed as he drifted off. Keith wanted to ask him *what now*? What they shared now was perfect, but he still had no idea where things stood between him and Dominic.

"There is no way for me to say this without it being awkward..." Keith began in a low voice to the man beside him before he could doze off.

Dominic

Dominic didn't know what to say. Obviously the memories were still painful, but other than empty words of condolences, he knew nothing he said would ease the pain. So he simply grabbed Keith's hand and tugged until the man lay closer to him.

Even as Dominic started to drift, some part of his brain heard Keith's softly spoken words. "There is no way for me to say this without it being awkward..." The seriousness of his tone caused Dominic to instantly wake and still as he waited for Keith to finish whatever he was about to say.

After a few tense seconds, Dominic sat up and blurted out, "Do you want me to leave?" He hoped his disappointment didn't bleed through. After that talk, he had felt that they had connected, but now he wondered if he had just imagined it.

Keith grabbed his arm, "What? No! No. That's not what I meant. I meant we should have discussed this before. I just need to know what you're looking to get from this," Keith said, motioning between them.

Dominic fidgeted; he had no idea how to ask for what he wanted without sounding pathetic. He didn't even know if it was possible to have a relationship in this environment. Dominic had seen more than his share of relationships fail during his time in the service. The stress of the job was often too much for a significant other to take.

"I'm not sure what we can have," he hedged, hoping that Keith would throw him a lifeline.

However, the look that flashed in his eyes let Dominic know that he had missed the mark entirely.

Scrambling to recover, Dominic quickly added, "How much do you want to give?"

Dominic knew exactly what he wanted, where he hoped things were headed between them. He had exactly zero experience in relationships, and all his brief encounters had been strictly one and done, so he wasn't sure where this left them.

Keith

Keith tried to follow his ramblings, but Dominic seemed determined to avoid answering a question. Sitting up, he reached over to turn on a light, and they both blinked as their night vision was distorted by the dim lighting. This was it: after weeks of waiting and wanting this man, Keith just had to put it out there and let it play itself out.

"I want to have a relationship. I want it to be more than just sex. I want to see where this leads. I think we could be good together." A ghost of a smile played on Dominic's face as Keith listed out exactly what he wanted, which he took as a good sign so he continued. "I realize you've never been with a man before, but I am not interested in hiding. We can take it as slow as you want, but I have been open about my sexuality for a long time."

After he finished his speech, Keith belatedly realized he might sound needy as fuck, but he really didn't care. He needed to know if Dominic was interested in what he was offering. There was no need to spend any more time fixated on the man if he was only up for a quick fuck.

Dominic

"Okay. But fair warning: I have no idea what I'm doing." Dominic smiled at the stunned expression Keith wore.

He figured Keith must have thought he would be more indecisive, but truthfully he wanted all the things Keith had said. He'd just never thought he could have them. He couldn't help but lean over and kiss those now-grinning lips.

The kiss started out nearly chaste, but it quickly gained momentum with each swipe of tongue. Dominic fisted both hands into Keith's unruly mane for balance as the man leaned into him and took control. Keith growled against his mouth before breaking the kiss.

"There is something else," Keith added sheepishly.

Dominic sat back up and waited for him to continue.

"I was kind of nosing into your past over the last two weeks," Keith confessed. "I wanted to get to know you, and the last two weeks you had been avoiding me. I was trying to find out if there was some reason, or some person in your life—"

"I know," Dominic interrupted.

As funny as it was watching the man squirm, Dominic decided to let him off the hook. He was surprised by Keith's honesty and that made him quick to forgive, although there was nothing in his past that he wanted to hide from Keith or his team.

"You knew?" Keith asked.

"Well, I didn't know it was you, but I was contacted last week about someone trying to access my records. I figured it was just someone on the team that was curious about the new guy. Either way, I didn't care then and I don't care now." Dominic ran his hands down Keith's chest towards the refueled erection he could see under the sheets. Leaning forward, he licked the pebbled nipple taunting him, sucking it in his mouth as he peered up at his lover.

"Fuck. Let's get some sleep," Keith mumbled as he not so discreetly adjusted himself beneath the sheet.

"What? Why do you want to stop?" Dominic's suddenly perky cock was more than interested in continuing. He again slid his palm across Keith's sheet-covered erection before he gripped it firmly. Keith groaned and gave a quick thrust before he buried his face in Dominic's neck.

"If we keep this up, I'm gonna want to get at you again and you will be sore in the morning." His voice was muffled as he spoke into Dominic's neck, his tongue flicking across a particularly sensitive spot with each word.

Dominic rolled to his side, dragging them both back flat onto the mattress. Dominic pressed their bodies together from chest to knees, and he gasped when their cocks settled in side by side.

"I don't care because now I need it." Dominic groaned as he humped up against Keith's erection.

Keith

"Fuck this," Keith growled as he slammed their lips together. The kiss was nearly violent as he rolled them, pinning Dominic to the bed. Reaching over his head, he located the lube that he had slid back under his pillow, but left the condoms behind.

Keith had no intention of fucking Dominic again that night, because he really didn't want the man to be sore for the following day's training exercise. But then again, he had no intention of leaving his man unsatisfied. He pulled back and poured an obscene amount of lube on his palm before Keith gripped both of their erections in his large hand.

"This will take the edge off, baby, but no fucking. I don't want to hurt you," he explained when it looked as if Dominic was going to complain. He squeezed their lengths together and tugged before the man could speak. Keith groaned when Dominic whimpered and pushed up off the bed, fucking into his fist and creating a dizzying amount of friction.

There was no way he could completely close his hand, not with both their cocks engorged. He could barely reach up to swipe the pad of his thumb over their tips. Even though his cock was slightly longer, Dominic's had a girth that made his asshole ache as he imagined being impaled by that beast. Resting on his elbow for better leverage, Keith quickened his strokes as Dominic began to thrust into his hand in earnest.

Keith knew this time wouldn't take long, and he doubted that Dominic had ever spent more than five minutes in a dark alley with a man, he truly had no idea how good it could be. It made Keith all the more determined to show him what he had been missing. He wanted to be Dominic's first and last everything.

Dominic

After another mind-bending orgasm, Dominic was unsure he could have remembered his own name as his body was racked with aftershocks. He had climaxed embarrassingly fast, his only comfort being that Keith had immediately followed him over the edge. The last thing he remembered was being gently wiped down.

Dominic awoke from an unusually restful night to find himself completely wrapped around Keith. He lay perfectly still and watched his handsome face for a few moments while listening to his soft snores.

Dominic wondered how exactly to extract himself from the tangle of limbs without waking him. After several unsuccessful attempts, he simply rolled the uncooperative man out of the way. His bladder was at full capacity and he would be pissing whether he made it to the bathroom or not.

"Good morning," Dominic said as he slid from the bed, noticing that Keith had woken instantly at the touch. Keith tensed briefly until he seemed to put a name to his new bedmate.

"Hey, baby," Keith replied. Dominic felt more than just a twinge in his backside as he padded naked across the room, his morning erection missing the memo that they were sated.

Breakfast first, Dominic reprimanded his overeager cock as Keith rolled from the bed, his tempting ass on display. It took a while for his cock to soften enough to piss, so by the time he began to rinse his mouth, Keith was staggering in to relieve his own full bladder.

"Hey, wanna grab a shower before chow?" Keith suggested as Dominic went to find his clothes. He sprinted to his room to grab some fresh gear and his shower kit and hurried back.

Showering together almost proved to be a very bad idea.

After he cleaned his body, Dominic ducked under the spray to deal with his too-long hair. He damn near bit off his tongue when his cock was unceremoniously swallowed to the root; he barely had time to brace himself against the wall before Keith had him up on his toes. *Holy shit!*

Keith sucked his cock like a man on a mission, his mouth and hands working in perfect concert as he alternated between caressing Dominic's balls and stroking the shaft. The suction increased as Keith went to play with his ass, distracting him completely before he slid a sneaky digit into his sore hole.

Dominic gripped Keith's shoulders as he was forced off balance. Those magic fingers nailed his prostate with amazing accuracy. Keith was obviously a master of multitasking, as he stroked his own cock at a breakneck pace; Dominic could just hear the rhythmic slapping over his own rapid breath.

In less than five minutes, Dominic had dumped his load down Keith's throat as he writhed on the fingers impaling him. Never had any single orgasm in the past completely devastated him, yet somehow that was what happened each time Keith wrecked his body in some way.

Even on his knees, Keith completely dominated everything; every touch seemed to brand Dominic, leaving him irrevocably claimed. Such was the case as Keith reached his own peak and came all over his legs, marking Dominic in the most primitive of ways. He was still shaking with the aftershocks when Keith swatted his ass hard.

"Let's go, babe. The Lieutenant will kill us if we're late." Keith stepped out of the shower and left the room. Ten minutes later they were dressed and headed towards the door. They barely had enough time to grab a quick bagel before rushing out to the training yard.

Dominic couldn't believe how much had changed in one night. "Are you planning on calling me babe in front of the team?" Dominic asked as they headed down the hall.

Keith stopped so suddenly Dominic nearly smacked into him. Keith turned, lifting up his shades. "Yes, actually, I was," he answered, lifting his eyebrow in challenge.

"Okay. I just wanted to be prepared if you did," Dominic answered honestly.

Dominic smiled as they continued out towards the armory for training. He was amazed that he had no issue with Keith calling him *baby* or *babe*. At first he had been surprised, but he'd quickly realized he enjoyed the affectionate moniker.

He had been called many things by many people over the years, most of them completely unflattering, but never had anyone used a term of endearment in reference to him. Even when his parents referred to him as their baby, the term had always seemed cutting.

But for some reason, when Keith said it, it made his heart beat wildly—funny how he had never considered himself the mushy type.

Maybe we're getting soft in our old age, his Angel snickered.

It was absolutely insane how much he was into this man. From the moment they'd met, Dominic had felt somehow completely drawn to him. He was never the type to believe in love at first sight, but now he had to wonder if there was such a thing.

Because what he felt was wholly different than the bouts of lust he had for other men over the years. Being with Keith just felt... right.

They walked toward the team already gathered around, chatting. Everyone was already bullshitting when they got there, and Dominic wondered how long it would take for them to detect the change in their relationship.

There was no hiding anything from a group of people who were trained to spot the smallest of details.

Dominic struggled not to fidget or draw any undue attention to the fact that they were standing together, slightly closer than some would deem necessary in casual company.

As Dominic joined the conversation about the live fire training, he noticed Steven's subtle smirk. Apparently, it had only taken him a second to spot the difference between them, but then again, he already knew that the possibility existed.

There was also Natasha, who just gave a ghost of a wink and continued on with her conversation with Sam as if nothing had happened; Dominic knew she would never betray the confidence of her best friend.

Of all their team members, Natasha was the one that Dominic felt the least connected to. At first, he thought it was because she had a barrier that he wasn't able to get through, but later he had to admit it was his jealousy. It was painfully obvious that Natasha and Keith were close friends, but Dominic had feared that maybe they were more than that.

Steven had nearly doubled over laughing when Dominic had suggested that they might be fucking. And though he had no reason, or right, to be jealous, he still had a hard time convincing his sometimes caustic Angel that slitting Natasha's throat was a bad idea.

Dominic could almost detect when each person realized that there was something going on with him and Keith. They each got that puppy dog look, their heads tilted and eyes narrowed as their gaze flicked from one to the other. Keith decided to remove any doubt the others might have had by placing his hand possessively on the small of Dominic's back.

"Alright, gentlemen. Today we are practicing urban live fire drills." Lucky quickly grabbed everyone's attention as he laid out the details of the training event.

Chapter 6

"Well, that went better than I thought it would," Dominic joked as they lay across his bed, exhausted and staring up at the ceiling. The training evolutions had gone off without a hitch, with everyone able to read each other's signals perfectly. Dominic had wondered if the others would react negatively to Keith's open display of affection.

Amazingly, not one person had seemed to care that they were obviously fucking like bunnies. Dominic had been prepared for side looks, whispered comments, or maybe even a full-on confrontation. But just like his confession on the rooftop with Steven, everyone had just shrugged and continued on as if the world hadn't just shifted, as if nothing had changed.

Each time Dominic had been paired off with a different agent, he had tensed, but the reaction he'd been expecting never came. By the time he was paired back up with Keith, he had realized that maybe he was truly surrounded by people who would accept him the way he was. No conditions, no judgments; they didn't treat him any differently than they had before. And that was something he would have to consider later…

"I don't know what you thought would happen, but these are good guys. Besides, I would never knowingly expose you to someone I thought might be a threat." Dominic had to bite back a groan at Keith's possessive tone, because for some reason, that really turned him on. He wasn't sure if it was the sense of belonging he felt when Keith talked like that or the fact that Keith obviously wanted him as much as he wanted Keith.

"Yeah well, I've met a lot of good guys that wouldn't hesitate to stomp the shit out of a couple of fags." Dominic winced at the harshness he could hear in his own voice, but he had seen more than one person get a beat down, or worse, for being gay. People he'd thought were tolerant and kind changed into horrible, vile excuses for human beings in the face of something that didn't fit with their views of normal.

The look on Keith's face was a picture of shock, and his reaction was immediate and expected. There was no way he could've figured out on his own why Dominic was so reluctant to let the others know he was gay. It wasn't his own shame per se, but he had seen what could happen to someone who was exposed. The consequences had been both quick and extreme, and Dominic would be lying if he denied that those events still shaped his beliefs today.

"Yeah, I've seen it happen." Keith nodded sadly. "But I'm not going to let other people's ignorance dictate how I live," he insisted. "And I'm not too worried about someone kicking my ass. Or trying to." He grinned brightly when Dominic rolled his eyes.

Dominic sat quietly as he mulled over what Keith had said. He was glad that he hadn't tried to minimize his experiences or how he felt.

Keith's insinuation that Dominic had allowed what other people thought to dictate how he lived his life was true. His self-imposed celibacy had robbed him the chance to have any type of meaningful relationships in the past, but now it seemed as if the fates had given him another chance. This time he'd do it right.

"Let's take a shower so I can reward you for your bravery today," Keith teased as he pulled off his shirt and headed towards the bathroom.

Dominic watched hungrily as Keith prowled across the room, each muscle rolling under his skin drawing his attention all over again. Fuck, the man was sexy. Dominic really couldn't figure out how he'd managed to land such a fine-ass man, but this was one gift horse he was not going to look in the mouth.

"Are you coming, babe?" Keith asked, kicking off his sweats. Dominic didn't need any further invitation; he jumped up and followed his lover to the bathroom, stripping as he went.

After their extra-long shower—with lots of unhelpful groping and Keith stroking Dominic off—Dominic made the unpleasant decision to chase Keith out with a promise to pick up where they left off. He stayed behind a few extra minutes to rinse the evidence of their activities from his already sweaty body. When he finally dried off and headed back to the room, he found the man fast asleep in his bed.

Huh. Guess we should have gotten out when he did. Looks like there won't be any fucking after all, his Angel complained.

Dominic shrugged and dropped his towel on the floor, uncaring of the mess. All he wanted was to join Keith on the bed. When he had done so, Dominic quickly following him into sleep.

As usual, Dominic's dreams pulled him back awake. This time it was not the usual dreams—or rather, nightmares—of the people he'd killed; tonight they were dreams of sex.

The best kind of sex—hot, dirty and unapologetic— his dreams were filled with hands, mouths, cocks, and cum. One after another, his dreams shifted from position to position, his body strung tight as he was sucked, fucked, and stroked to completion, time and time again.

The background changed. Sometimes they were on a bed, and sometimes he was draped across a table or pressed against the wall of the shower. But each had the same effect; he felt heat pooling in his belly like he never had before, hot and all encompassing.

He bit back a groan as he woke, shifting. His cock was already leaking and his balls pulled up tight, aching with a need created by his unconscious mind. Dominic stretched, and he felt Keith's erection as it pressed up against his ass.

All his previous sexual encounters with men had ended without him reciprocating. Even with Keith, he hadn't really given back yet. He had never really wanted to before now, but as he felt Keith's cock lying tantalizingly on his backside, he could admit to himself that the thought had his mouth watering.

Dominic turned slowly in Keith's arms so as not to wake him; he looked at his sleeping face, so relaxed in that moment, then he scooted lower on the bed, carefully so as not to wake his unsuspecting target, until the object of his desire was right in front of his face. He hesitated, not sure what to do now he was here, not sure if he'd be welcome.

Just do it! No man has ever complained about waking up to his dick being sucked, his Angel whispered in encouragement.

Firmly grasping Keith's dick, the first thing that Dominic noticed was how similar Keith's felt to his own, the soft flesh like velvet over steel. Although this was the first dick, other than his own, that he had ever touched— and the first dick he'd had the intention of sucking— Dominic realized he was eager for a taste.

Having been on the receiving end of a blowjob or several, he knew how good it felt to be wrapped in that perfect combination of suction and wet heat. He hesitated. Would he be any good at it?

Dominic looked up when he heard Keith's pained declaration. "You are thinking way too much, baby. Trust me, I'll like anything you do."

Keith had evidently guessed Dominic's train of thought, but there was something about the way he sounded that made Dominic's cock jerk. Like he was desperate, on edge. Almost begging. It was intoxicating. Stroking up to the tip, Dominic slowly licked across the engorged head, a burst of salty, bittersweet fluid exploding in his mouth.

As the taste rolled across his tongue, Dominic's cock throbbed and a bead of pre-cum slid down his shaft. A quick glance up and his pulse quickened as Keith stared down at him, face tinged pink with arousal.

Dominic licked the sensitive bundle of nerves behind the tip, the way he knew drove him crazy when someone did it to him. "I have no idea what I'm doing. I've never sucked a cock before," Dominic admitted, whispering.

Keith bucked his hips at the action as he gritted out, "Shit, babe. Keep doing that. Just knowing my cock is the only one that's ever been in your mouth makes this the best fucking head I've ever had." Keith was so serious in his assertion that Dominic knew that he would never regret Keith being his first.

A need to taste more inspired him to suck the tip into his mouth, lavishing attention on it as he would an ice-pop in the middle of summer. Dominic was rewarded with another bead of pre-cum. A low moan only made Dominic suck harder, he wanted Keith to feel a fraction of the pleasure the man always gave him.

"Don't stop, babe. Take me deeper," Keith groaned as he gently threaded his fingers into Dominic's hair.

Dominic had been thinking of going to town to get his hair trimmed; he hadn't gone since a week before he got to the Hive. But each time Keith tugged at the strands, a fresh wave of desire spiked through him, and Dominic thought he might just keep it longer.

He dipped his head and attempted to take as much of the thick cock as he possibly could. Saliva coated over his own hand, and he took even more into his mouth, which triggered his gag reflex and made him cough and drool.

"Fuck, yes. Just like that, babe. Just remember to breathe through your nose and when I touch the back of your throat, try to swallow," Keith suggested, his voice wavering with the effort to talk. His thighs trembled as he held himself in check.

Dominic followed his instructions; he concentrated on his breathing, his head bobbed up and down. He used his hand to slowly stroke the parts his lips didn't cover. He experimented with suction—twirling his tongue around the tip, taking him deeper each time. This time when he felt Keith touch the back of his throat, he forced himself to swallow.

Keith cussed. "God... Yes... fuck, babe, just like that. I want to feel you gagging on my dick." Keith spread his legs wider and tightened his grip in Dominic's hair while he thrust gently. "I'm getting so close, babe..." Keith warned.

Dominic applied more suction. When he felt Keith's hips stutter, he had no intention of pulling back. No, he wanted it all; he wanted to know what the man would taste like, and he wanted to feel that cock in his mouth twitch and spill its load all over his tongue.

Keith let out a ragged groan as he realized that Dominic was going to swallow him down. Dominic tentatively cupped a hand around his balls and that seemed to make Keith's patience snap.

Holding on tight, Keith shoved roughly into Dominic's mouth until he hit the back of his throat; it made him gag and he struggled to swallow him further. Keith pulled back slightly, his balls pulling up tight under Dominic's chin right before his cock pulsed, squeezing out spurt after spurt of hot liquid and filling Dominic's mouth.

Although he had been expecting it, somehow the force and sheer volume of Keith's climax still surprised him. It wasn't the warm, salty taste as much as it was the struggle to swallow it all. And he was absolutely shocked when his own orgasm slammed through him in response, coating the sheets beneath him, without anyone even touching his dick. That was a first too.

He laid his head on Keith's hip as they both recovered. After a few minutes Keith began to chuckle. Looking up, Dominic arched his eyebrow in question. "What's so funny?" he asked.

Keith gently stroked his hair as he sobered. "I have no idea what inspired your impromptu performance, but I am eternally grateful for whatever it was."

Dominic could feel a blush creep up his neck as the inspiration came to the forefront of his mind. But there was no way he was about to admit that he had dreamt about sucking Keith's dick; that sounded perverted even in his own mind.

So instead he offered, "I've wanted to do that to you for a while. It's just that I've never done it before. It took a while to build up the nerve." Which was the truth for the most part; he had been thinking about sucking Keith's dick, and more, ever since that first kiss.

Keith smiled. "Well, baby, I have to say that was fucking mind blowing and any time you feel like doing that again, for practice or whatever, I will be more than happy to play test subject." Keith's smile was wicked as he wiggled his hips playfully.

Chapter 7

Dominic ~ January, Pennsylvania

Their first official date had ended in disaster. Dominic wanted to enjoy a romantic evening with Keith outside of the Hive.

"I'm sure everybody has finished dinner. How about we grab some food and maybe hit the mall to catch a movie?" Keith suggested as they each got dressed and went to brush their teeth.

Dominic nodded with his toothbrush in his mouth; this was so strange, the normalcy of it all. He couldn't help but be amazed as they moved around each other as if they had been doing so for years. At thirty-five, he had his first boyfriend; he was not sure how long this would last, but he felt more comfortable in his own skin than he ever had before.

They hit the mall in Scranton, grabbing a quick bite to eat in one of the nondescript chain restaurants. Dominic tried to relax and enjoy the meal, but he couldn't help but wonder if the other patrons could tell that they were together. He knew he was being ridiculous, but that didn't dispel the knot in his chest as he tried to appear calm.

"Hey, you okay?" Keith asked and Dominic realized that Keith had noticed how tense he became the moment they got out of the car. All the carefree conversations had dried up as he'd set his shoulders in a rigid posture and all but marched into the restaurant.

"Yeah," Dominic said and he could see Keith practically biting his tongue to not interrogate him.

They finished their meal in an uncomfortable silence, and Dominic wondered for the hundredth time if he had made a mistake rushing them out into public as he paid the tab. They headed towards the cinema and out of nowhere, Keith reached out to touch Dominic.

Dominic flinched and Keith pulled back, obviously taking his reflexive response as a rejection. The tension between them was so thick Dominic felt it as a tangible force that wedged between them. They reached the cinema, received their tickets, and went inside. They spent the entire time as if they were complete strangers. After two of the longest hours of his life, Dominic was grateful to head immediately to the vehicle.

The strain continued for the first twenty minutes of the ride back, until Keith turned in his seat to face him.

"I'm sorry." His voice was pained with a hint of shame, and Dominic felt a stab of regret at the torment in his eyes.

"You have nothing to be sorry for, babe. I shouldn't have rushed this." He desperately wanted Keith to know that he wanted this and how much he appreciated how patient Keith has been, but changing a lifetime of behavior was not going to be easy for him.

"Can you just have patience with me? Let me get my head used to the idea?" Dominic asked with trepidation, exposing his fear that Keith would soon tire of being with someone who could not offer him the kind of relationship Keith deserved.

Keith offered him a smile as he said, "Take all the time you need, babe. I'm not going anywhere."

That had been over a month ago, and Dominic had made several comments about wanting them to go out to town again. Each time Keith had deflected, instead claiming he was fine with only being out in a safe place with their friends. Now that their relationship had some strength and time behind it, Dominic felt it was time to try that date again.

The team had been given the entire weekend off. Although Keith and Dominic spent every night together, they'd rarely had time outside of the Hive to be together romantically as a couple. Keith was changing that tonight. He'd made dinner reservations at a nice Japanese restaurant that he had been meaning to check out.

Although their relationship had been progressing steadily, Dominic still had moments when he would tense when Keith reached for him in public. It wasn't that he was ashamed of their relationship, but a few months of happiness did not erase years of hiding. He promised himself that tonight he would relax no matter what.

Keith deserved to have a man who could hold his hand without first checking to see who may be watching. That first date had been a failure on an epic scale, and Dominic had sworn that the next time would be different. Keith never called him out on it, but each time he flinched, even though they were just at home around friends, he would still sometimes react. Dominic could see ·the disappointment in Keith's eyes each time before he buried it with a wink or his sexy smirk.

Dominic dressed in his charcoal slacks with matching top and jacket, opting to go without a tie. Keith had mentioned that the restaurant was formal but he hoped not tie formal. He had nothing against dressing up, but suit ties always made him feel like he was dressing for a funeral. He questioned the need for his sidearm, but in the end he tucked it in his shoulder holster.

It's better to have it and not need it, than need it and not have it, his Angel agreed as he stepped outside to pick up his date.

Dominic stood slack-jawed when Keith opened the door. He was dressed in stark contrast, favoring all lighter colors. He looked devastatingly handsome in his light tan slacks and jacket with an artic-white top. Having also foregone a tie, he left his hair from his normal ponytail, his long blond hair fell mid-way down his back.

Dominic had the urge to say *fuck the date* and drag the man back into the bedroom. "Hey, babe. You look great." Keith leered.

Taking a breath, Dominic gave his randy dick a mental slap down. "So do you," he replied and he gave his man a chaste kiss.

"You ready to get out of here?" Keith asked as he locked his door. By the looks that Keith was giving him, they might never leave the building if they didn't leave then.

"Lead the way, sweetheart," Dominic said as they headed towards the garage.

They talked the entire drive to Binghamton, the conversation moving from music to sports to politics; they shared similar tastes and views. Keith had never been with someone that he could be one hundred percent honest with. People said he should never date a coworker, but when he worked as a government assassin, dating one of his own was turning out to be the best idea.

Pulling into the parking garage, Keith laughed when they both pulled their handguns to check the clips. Once out of the vehicle, Dominic proceeded to surprise the hell out of Keith by immediately grabbing his hand as they walked towards the street. That was how they continued down the busy street towards the restaurant, hand-in-hand.

"Do you have a reservation, gentlemen?" the hostess asked as soon as they walked into the finely-decorated establishment. Keith spoke with the hostess as Dominic took in his surroundings; this place had the appearance of a traditional Geisha house.

They took off their shoes as directed before they followed her to the seating area, where the tables were low to the ground and pillows served as seats. "Wow. Keith, this place is amazing. Have you ever been here before?" Dominic asked as he arranged himself at the table.

Keith chuckled as he took his seat. The lighting was dim and tea candles flickered around the room, providing an intimate feel. Although there were several other patrons, the way the room was separated implied they were alone. "No, but I'd read about it and was always waiting for the opportunity to experience it."

The waitress returned with their menus and a bottle of rice sake. "Gentlemen, your tea service will begin while you decide your meal."

She bowed as a small, intricately dressed woman appeared. Neither man spoke as they watched the age-old ritual performed before their eyes. By the end, when she took their order, it was safe to assume that they would be back.

"Damn, that was impressive," Keith stated as their food began to arrive.

"Yeah, I've never seen anything like it." Dominic's plate was set down in front of him. They ate and chatted about the latest video game Steven had somehow gotten them all addicted to.

"Would you like some dessert?" Keith asked once they had cleared their plates.

Dominic flushed, "Yes, but we have to go home to have it." Keith had his credit card out before the waitress handed him the bill.

"Whatever the bill is, add a twenty percent tip," Keith said, handing her the card as he got to his feet. "We'll be at the door."

Dominic chuckled as he got to his feet to follow the very eager spook. It didn't happen often, but Dominic just loved when he shocked Keith. By the time he made it over to grab his shoes, Keith was completely dressed and signing the slip. Dominic took his time putting on his shoes and coat.

Nothing wrong with prolonging the tease, his Angel agreed.

But as they headed back to the garage, Dominic couldn't shake the feeling of being watched. One look at Keith confirmed that sensation in his gut. They both stayed alert, their gazes sweeping, swallowing entire areas as they searched for the eyes that they could feel on them. "Switch," he said barely over a whisper.

"Yeah, I feel it too. Let's just get back to the car," Keith replied, his voice just as low. They lengthened their stride slightly; if they had a tail, the person would have to match their cadence to keep up and break their cover.

When they reached the vehicle, whoever had been on their six had eased back. Keith did a quick sweep of the car, ensuring there had been no tampering while they had been away. He gave the all clear; they slid in and started on their way back to the Hive.

"Was probably nothing," Keith chuckled, although his voice was tight and held no humor.

"Yeah," Dominic agreed, but still he found himself checking the mirrors for any sign of a pursuit vehicle.

"I'm going to make a few loops to make sure it was nothing," Keith answered his unasked question as he turned off in the opposite direction.

After twenty minutes of misdirection, they headed back towards the Hive. "Hey, Keith, thanks for tonight. It was really great," Dominic offered as he relaxed. Apparently they'd both spent a little too much time in the field; they were constantly paranoid that someone was always watching.

It's not paranoia if everyone is *out to kill you,* his Angel reminded him quickly.

Keith reached over and twined their fingers together, "You're welcome, baby." He pulled their joined hands to his mouth to brush a kiss on Dominic's hand. Even with that nagging feeling in the back of his mind, Dominic couldn't help but shiver as lust coiled deep in his belly.

When they returned to the Hive, Dominic noticed that most of the team was still out enjoying their break. He gave up a silent thanks to whatever God might hear because he wanted no distractions tonight.

Dominic fumbled with the key as he tried for the third time to open his door. Keith had been on him nonstop since they reached the Hive. The fact the man in question was palming his cock through his pants and nibbling his ear was doing zero good for his hand-eye coordination.

"Open the door, baby, unless you want me to fuck you in the hall," Keith teased before he bit down on that flesh between Dominic's shoulder and neck. Keith had discovered early that it was an especially sensitive area, and he exploited this knowledge shamelessly.

They tumbled into the room when the door finally opened and Keith spun Dominic, pressing him into the wall as he kicked the door shut. "Now where were we? Ah, yes, I remember now," Keith announced before ripping off both their jackets.

Dominic sucked in a breath as Keith's hands fluttered around the hem of his shirt. In a blur of movement, the garment was removed, almost taking his nose with it. Keith dropped to his knees and licked a trail down Dominic's belly while his hands masterfully unbuckled his belt. The zipper sounded impossibly loud over their raspy breath. Then his pants hit the ground.

Keith mouthed Dominic's cock through his boxers while encouraging him to lift his leg. One after the other, his shoes and socks were removed as Keith continued to nuzzle his balls through that annoying piece of fabric. Once he was completely naked, Keith stood. Dominic whimpered a protest as his cock was completely ignored.

"What's the matter, baby? Don't like the tease?" Keith asked as he slowly removed his shirt. Dominic groaned as he reached for his own cock.

If he wants to play, I'll just take care of myself.

Keith gripped his wrist. "Oh no, baby. That belongs to me."

Keith's smile was pure evil as he walked around Dominic, still holding his wrist.

"I want you on the bed face down, waiting for me," Keith purred in his ear as he ground his covered erection on Dominic's naked ass. "Can you do that for me?" Keith asked as he stepped back and waited.

Dominic wanted to scream *no!* but he knew the pleasure would be that much better if he played this game out until the end. "Yes!" Dominic hissed in frustration as he headed towards the bed as he was directed.

"Good boy. Wait for me. I have to grab some supplies." Keith chuckled as he opened the door and headed to his room.

Dominic groaned as he sprawled prone on his mattress, down like ordered. It would be so easy to just hump the mattress for relief, but when had he ever liked easy? Anxiety and anticipation churned in his gut as he watched Keith enter the room. Without a word Keith prowled towards him, Dominic tried to focus on relaxing as his breath hitched and pulse sped up in anticipation.

Keith

Keith firmly grabbed Dominic's ankles and jerked his legs apart. He took a moment to appreciate the powerful man that chose to submit this way. Keith placed gentle kisses down Dominic's spine as he began kneading and massaging his thighs.

Keith licked a path from the top of Dominic's ass to his shoulders, pausing to leave little bites on his neck and ears. Keith chuckled as Dominic moaned and spread his legs in response. Keith pushed his knees between Dominic's spread legs and massaged his ass, pushing his cheeks together and pulling them back apart. Keith growled, watching Dominic's asshole clench rhythmically—looking so eager to be filled.

Keith continued to move at an excruciatingly slow pace, squeezing Dominic's ass in a hold just this side of painful. He pushed Dominic's cheeks up and together then pulled them obscenely wide apart. Keith gripped Dominic's hips and tugged, encouraging Dominic to lift up on his knees. Keith resumed his ministrations, teasing, pulling his ass apart, this time he dipped in and swiped his tongue across Dominic's hole.

"Fuck!" Dominic gasped as he scrambled for purchase, damn near leaping off the bed. Keith chuckled; he had anticipated that move and held Dominic's hips steady with a vise-like grip. Now that he was sure that the man would not be getting away, Keith set about his mission of taking Dominic completely apart.

Keith began by slowly licking across that tight muscle, making sure his tongue was flat, covering every inch of flesh. Keith sucked and nibbled the tender flesh until he heard Dominic's guttural moan. He pointed his tongue and pushed through those tight muscles quickly, then he blew across the drenched skin with another soft breath.

Keith stiffened his tongue as he circled that wrinkled muscle, pushing and sucking, keeping him wet. "Don't move," Keith ordered as he released his restraining hold on one hip so he could get his fingers in the game. Using just one spit-soaked finger, he petted Dominic's hole until the muscle started to push out, softening enough to slide in to the first knuckle.

Keith had to take a deep breath to beat back his own need to get inside that tight hole; his man still needed to be prepped slowly. Although they had been fucking almost nightly, Dominic was still impossibly tight. Licking around his finger, Keith gently pulled down on that tight ring to open him up. Once the resistance lessoned, he pulled his finger free and replaced it with his tongue.

Dominic's breathing became labored, signaling his impending orgasm. Determined to push him over the edge, Keith sucked on the fingers of his free hand as he continued to stroke Dominic's cock. He pushed in one finger, quickly followed by the second. Curling them, he rubbed Dominic's prostate hard as he quickly pumped his cock. Dominic cussed and slammed back hard as ropes of ejaculate streamed from his cock. Keith quickly pulled his fingers free as Dominic collapsed on the bed.

Keith stroked his own cock with his cum-covered hand before covering his lover's body with his own. He slid his cock between Dominic's legs, desperate for the friction that would send him over the edge. It wouldn't take much or long, he was more than halfway there just from feeling Dominic come undone. Feeling his balls pull up tight, Keith sped up his thrusts; when Dominic squeezed his cock tightly between his thighs, Keith's own orgasm slammed into him out of nowhere.

Dominic

Dominic had fought not to squirm as sharp teeth sank into his ass cheeks, one at a time, and roaming fingers brushed his opening. There was always a price to pay for all the pleasure Keith could give him. Without warning, a wet tongue flicked over Dominic's puckered flesh as Keith blew a puff of air across his hole.

Dominic's entire body fluttered with sensation. His sphincter tightened and released as Keith lightly tapped his tongue directly on his hole. Dominic moaned and cursed as he tried to push back against his face in need of something… Anything to scratch that itch that grew by the second. His orgasm slowly built off in the distance. He just needed a little more to bring it to the surface.

Dominic bucked and groaned before he dropped his chest to the bed. He knew what was coming, and even though he wanted it, there was always a moment when his body locked up tight, resisting the intrusion.

Dominic pushed back driving him in deeper. "Oh. My. Fucking… God… Keith!" Dominic yelled as he ground against Keith's face. Keith used his free right hand to grip Dominic's cock and stroke.

Keith took multi-tasking to mind numbingly good levels as he jacked Dominic's cock while jabbing relentlessly at his prostate. Dominic didn't know if he wanted to run away from the dual onslaught or shove down harder. The decision was taken from him when his orgasm came out of nowhere, nearly blinding him in its intensity as he slammed his head on the mattress.

He couldn't have helped if he tried as he watched Keith jerk himself off over him. His body was as useless as if he had run a marathon as the echoes of bliss reverberated through his core. Nothing had ever made him feel like this, and if he went by the way Keith bit off his name as he painted Dominic's chest with his jizz, it was safe to say he felt the same.

Although the meal had been fantastic, the small portions followed by vigorous fucking weren't enough. They were both starved as they recovered. Dominic rolled over to look at the clock, a groan ripped from him when he saw it was nearly 2 a.m. He turned back to his lover, "Hey, babe, I'm starving. Let's go grab something to eat."

"Well, everyone from our team should be gone for the night, so there should be some of last night's leftovers left in the fridge," Keith agreed as he got up in search of his clothes. "Hey, we can watch that movie I got last week," he added as they headed towards the door.

They raided the fridge and found a pot of leftover pasta and some steaks in containers. They heated up their makeshift meal and sat together at the table. The food quickly disappeared as they recounted their training mission, going over points and flaws they had noticed.

Dominic was pleased by how they could seamlessly transition from lovers to operatives; that had been one of his greatest concerns starting this relationship, especially while being the one on the receiving end. He had feared that Keith would treat him somehow lesser in regards to his job.

"You ready to watch that movie?" Keith asked as they cleaned up their dishes. "You know, we could watch some porn and fuck around. That room is completely soundproof," he added salaciously.

Dominic hummed his approval as Keith reached around to grip Dominic's more-than-interested cock.

As they quietly made their way to the entertainment room, Keith stopped short in the doorway. There, just over Keith's shoulder, Dominic could make out the sight of two bodies moving together on the couch. As he inched forward he noticed the shape of the body on top, and immediately Dominic knew it was a female.

Dominic couldn't pull his eyes away from the erotic display. It wasn't the sex—he had no interest in females sexually—but the passion burning between the two was damn near palpable. These were two people in love. Hushed words reached across the room as the lovers' movements became frantic.

This was private; this was intimate in a way that surpassed the act itself. His brain urged him to flee, but his feet remained frozen in place until Keith tugged him into motion. Dominic went to step back and bumped into the wall, making enough noise to alert the couple to their presence.

The bodies scrambled, trying to cover themselves although neither Keith nor Dominic could make out their faces in the pitch black room. Their surprise must have made them hesitate at the door a second too long, because a pissed-off voice hissed, "Get. The. Fuck. Out!"

Holy shit, that was Natasha!

Keith

"What the…" Keith started, his words cutting off as Dominic dragged him down the hall. "Dominic. That was fucking Natasha," Keith whispered.

Keith's mind reeled as he tried to piece together what they had just witnessed. Natasha would be the first to tell him that she was a veritable slut; she preferred nameless, faceless encounters.

On missions, she was one of their go-to people when the op called for getting close to their target. Men, women, it didn't much matter; she could seduce anyone with a pulse, and she was good at her job.

Her one rule that she never broke was that she never had a relationship with anyone she had to work with. It had been part of every speech she had given him to warn him away from pursuing Dominic: "Never shit where you eat."

It was ironic that Natasha had chosen to remind him of how awkward it had been when she'd had ended the sex arrangement she had with Sam over the last few weeks. And that had been purely string-free sex. What was going on in the theater, that hadn't looked like some one-off fuck.

Dominic

Dominic snatched Keith from the room before he could finish whatever the fuck he had been about to say. They had interrupted Natasha fucking somebody, and Dominic had no intention to stick around for the fireworks. He didn't stop moving until they were outside Keith's door.

"Do you want to talk about it?" Dominic asked as they went into the room. Keith rubbed his palm over his face and grimaced at the thought.

"No. As a matter of fact, I never want to talk about what we just saw again," he answered with a look on his face that bordered on pissed beyond all reason.

Dominic didn't know what to do with that response. His first reaction was suspicion. Why was Keith so upset that she was fucking someone? Did he have a thing for her? He dismissed that thought immediately. First, Keith was gay. He had never had, nor had he ever wanted to have, sex with a woman and, second, they were like siblings. No, there was something else going on with that situation, and Dominic wasn't entirely sure he wanted to know what it was.

"She was constantly telling me how getting involved with someone that we worked with on a daily basis was a terrible idea. She was the reason I hesitated for those two weeks in the beginning. I didn't want to risk the job," Keith confessed as they lay in bed.

Dominic was surprised Keith was willing to share this. Although he had known that Shock had not been his biggest fan in the beginning, some of their awkward encounters suddenly made sense; Natasha had always seemed to be watching him. Dominic had felt she was judging him, looking for something. At least this proved he wasn't paranoid.

"She knew that if we got together, it would be more than just fucking for me. Natasha and Sam had a fuck buddy thing that started back when we joined the team. She ended things a few weeks back."

Dominic stayed quiet, trying to piece together the story. He couldn't help the happiness that shot through him with the realization that Keith had never only wanted a physical relationship. This was not the time to focus on that, though; he needed to focus on giving Keith a place to vent. Dominic was convinced that it was a member of their team. They were the only people with access to that theater since all the other teams were in the field.

"So catching her fucking someone else we work with not only surprised me, but pissed me off. She harassed me nonstop about the mistake I was making with you and risking the entire team. Well, I guess whoever was fucking her stupid must be the exception." Keith's voice dripped with disdain and Dominic wondered if this revelation would damage Keith and Natasha's friendship permanently.

"Because I know Natasha and how she operates, and what we saw was not just her fucking someone. So yeah, I'm extra pissed. Not only did she try to keep us apart, but now I find out she's been lying to me. This makes me question our friendship in its entirety," Keith finished. The stress and hurt of Natasha's betrayal was obvious by the pained look on his face.

"Baby, I have no idea what she was doing, but I am sure being with whomever that was must be a decision she didn't make lightly," Dominic guessed. "Maybe seeing us together has given her the courage to pursue someone." He kissed Keith gently until he felt him relax.

"Thanks, babe. I want you to be right, maybe I'll talk to her about it tomorrow. We both need some time to cool down and process what happened." Keith pulled him into a tight embrace, and Dominic sighed in relief.

Dominic closed his eyes and took stock of everything that Keith had confessed. While he hadn't been particularly surprised by Natasha's feelings, it still stung. She had done everything in her power to keep them apart. It hadn't worked, but the fact that she had tried agitated him slightly.

Though he had to admit, although it would only be to himself, that she was a great friend to Keith. She would do anything to protect him. And that fact alone made her okay in Dominic's book. Well, actually, that made her more than okay. He would kill to have a friend as loyal as her.

Before sleep claimed him, he thought of Steven— they had become great friends, maybe not to the level of Switch and Shock, but Dominic thought of his partner as a brother, and although no words had been spoken he was sure his partner felt the same. So maybe he had a friend like that already, and that thought made him smile as he drifted off.

"Hey, babe, I'm going to need to talk to Natasha."

Dominic peered up at him with concern etched across his face. Glancing at the clock, Dominic groaned when he realized it was barely six in the morning. "Keith, are you sure you want to do this now? I know you are pissed and want to confront her, but you have been friends for a long time."

Keith

Keith was touched that Dominic was concerned about saving his friendship with the woman who had basically tried to keep them apart. But he knew that if he put this off, it would only make things worse. "Yeah, I'm sure."

Keith brushed their lips together for a brief kiss before he rolled out of the bed and headed for the shower. One way or another, he and Natasha would be putting this thing to bed. There was more than a friendship at stake: she was like his sister, someone he trusted with his life. So to learn that maybe she didn't trust him was heartbreaking.

After a quick shower, Keith got dressed and headed next door. Natasha was already dressed and sitting at her desk when he walked in, no doubt waiting for this conversation. While he knew it had to be settled, there was no real way to predict how it would end.

"Good morning, *mladshiy brat.* I imagine you've come because of last night, correct?" Natasha said, never one to beat around the bush.

"What do you think?" Keith growled, "So I guess your rules are more flexible than you led me to believe."

"Keith, I have wanted to talk to you many times about this, but the person I am seeing wasn't ready for the team to know."

"So you just lied to me for God knows how long to keep your lover's secret? Fuck, I thought we were like family, Natasha. So was this going on while you were warning me away from Dominic?"

"No! God no, Keith I am sorry for interfering with you and Dominic. I am even sorrier that I hid things from you." Natasha paced in front of the door. "I want to tell you everything, from the beginning, *mladshiy brat*. I will do anything to regain your trust and love, but what I tell you cannot leave this room. Agreed?"

"I won't hide this from Dominic."

Natasha paced a few more laps before agreeing. "Fine, *mladshiy brat*, let's start from the beginning."

Chapter 8

Dominic

The mission had been going like clockwork. With everyone in position, Lucky gave Keith, Sam, and Natasha the go ahead. As he entered the building, the hairs on the back of Dominic's neck stood up as they scanned the too-quiet room, the smell of bleach making his eyes and throat burn.

Someone's gone through a whole lot of trouble to cover their tracks, his Angel noted, and he had to agree.

The targets had spent a good amount of time ensuring they didn't leave any trace of evidence behind. *But how did they know to clean house?* They cleared the first room and quietly made their way down the hall, time slowed down as his brain registered the scent coming from the next room… blood, human blood, and lots of it.

Dominic glanced at Keith and Sam and realized they also detected the odor and were signaling for him to continue. He spoke softly into his mic, reporting their progress as they cleared each room. Coming to the opening beyond the last empty room, time ceased to exist as they found them… And each girl had a single gunshot wound to the head, discarded like unwanted trash with their bodies littering the floor of the gutted-out building.

As they checked every crevice, they received the all-clear. Other than the bodies, there was not a single trace of the human trafficking ring. They had somehow cleared out, taking everything with them. Sledge bit off a vicious string of profanities as he covered the body of a very pregnant young girl.

Keith pulled out his camera and began the unpleasant task of documenting the scene. There was no one here to apprehend, but worse yet, there was no one left to save. They had come into this with the purpose of saving these women from the sex slave industry; everyone had been on board for what was seen more as a rescue mission. But as he cataloged the twenty-four dead bodies, the fact that the mission was a complete and total failure was brutally driven home.

Lucky called in the recovery team to collect the bodies and any trace evidence left behind. It was merely a formality; the place had been sanitized. Every piece of furniture had been moved and by the smell of it, every standing surface had been bleached. The only thing left behind were the girls. It seemed impossible that they had decided to move at that precise moment. The intelligence had suggested that this had been a semi-permanent setup.

So what spooked them into running?

Dominic had a hard time believing that coincidence was behind the perfect timing of their escape. The surveillance teams had pulled away less than twenty-four hours ago, and somehow they had chosen that moment to go ghost. Something just didn't seem right. He caught part of Lucky's screaming orders to secure the scene and call in the surveillance team.

Seems like we're not the only ones that don't like this rendition of the perfect getaway, his Angel piped in.

He nearly jumped when Keith grabbed his shoulder. "Fuck, man. I'm gonna tie a bell around your fucking neck," Dominic grumbled. It was amazing that a man Keith's size could move so quietly.

"Ha! If you had said my balls I would have been interested, but I'll pass on the collar," Keith fired back as the humor returned to his haunted eyes. Dominic's face warmed, knowing the others could hear their dirty banter.

"The FBI is here, so we are rounding up to go to the airfield." Dominic tried to shake off the unease he felt about the entire situation; he would wait until they got home to discuss his take on the case. He grabbed his gear and followed Keith to the waiting van, suddenly grateful they had a private plane to take them back.

Halfway to the airport they received a radio transmission that they had a lead on the men suspected of running the sex ring. They were trying to sneak back to Russia via a cargo ship, and the team had the go-ahead to stop them by any means necessary.

Although relations with Russia were friendly at the moment and they would likely be permitted to pursue them there, the CIA had no intention of allowing these criminals off American soil. Now that the sex slavers had been upgraded to mass murderers, the team had received permission to hunt them down.

They raced to the Virginia shipping port; transmissions reported that a second team was already en route. Dominic and Steven prepped their rifles as Keith and the rest of the team checked their weapons and vests.

They arrived at the dock a few seconds ahead of the backup vehicle. As they exited the vehicle, each team member checked and rechecked the assortment of weapons they had strapped on their bodies.

Natasha

Normally, Natasha had no problem staying detached from the cases she worked on, but this one threatened to take her back to a situation she had barely escaped from the first time.

She and her sister had been forced to watch as their parents were brutally murdered. Their parents had tried to hide them when the masked men stormed the house, and the fight that transpired was short and brutal. Their father had been the first to die as he'd tried to negotiate for his family. After that, their mother had been quick to go on the offensive.

During the struggle, their mother had somehow knocked the knife from one of her attacker's hands. The men had been on her instantly with their fists and hands swinging wildly, and it had seemed like only seconds had passed before their mother's screams were silenced.

Vera had grabbed the fallen knife and stabbed the one closest man in his neck. When he fell to the ground, the second attacker had grabbed her from behind by the throat and slammed her to the ground before stabbing her in the chest with his knife.

The entire time she had stood there frozen, but seeing her sister twitch on the ground was enough to make her lose it. She had crawled over to the dying man and ripped out the knife still protruding from his throat. Without thought, she'd leapt on her sister's attacker and plunged the knife into his neck over and over until they both hit the ground. She remembered all too vividly struggling to climb out from under the man and crawl to her sister.

"Run," Vera had choked out as blood filled her mouth. "Run, baby, and don't trust anyone." Those are the last words she ever heard Vera speak as she'd turned around and ran.

Lucky

"The plan is to take the boat and kill anyone who tries to interfere." Lucky had jumped-to when the surveillance team told them the cargo ship used for smuggling girls was slated for departure in six hours.

Satellite imaging confirmed the suspects arriving at the ship and loading various items into shipping containers. This was, no doubt, all the evidence they had removed while gutting their stash house.

Grabbing twenty FBI and CIA agents, Lucky rerouted his team over the radio before he received the go-ahead from command. There was no way they were losing these bastards. Setting up a perimeter, they impatiently waited for satellite imaging to confirm the number of targets. After just under two hours, command confirmed fifteen targets in the lower compartments and five up top.

Dominic, Steven, Keith, and two FBI snipers set up on shipping containers; they were set to take out each top target simultaneously, giving the ground troops a clear entrance on the boat and ensuring no reinforcements could surprise them upon exit.

They made their approach in utter silence, pressing the element of surprise. Once they were in position, the snipers could clear the path to the lower levels. The CIA wanted as many detained as possible, but that was second to ensuring no one escaped.

Using the crates set for loading as cover, Lucky signaled to the sniper team that they were ready to go. It was a matter of seconds before Chaos reported back that all targets had been secured. Giving the signal, they fanned out and converged on the ship.

Making their way across the hull, Lucky led his men to the area that imaging had shown as being the staircase. Moving silently, they cleared each area they passed on their way to the lower cargo and living area. Lucky held back, slowing their pace, as they approached the closed double doors that opened to the cargo area.

Lucky signaled for the team to prepare to enter the room, and they broke into two teams one on either door. Lucky and his team would fan to the left while the other team secured the right side. Lucky pulled his weapon to the ready, signaling the go-on-three countdown.

Dominic

Dominic and his sniper team sat in complete silence and scanned the area for any threats as they waited for the situation report from the ground team. They all perked up at the *all secure* transmission. Lucky radioed command, advising that there were five additional bodies and two injured; the rest had surrendered quietly.

Dominic wasn't sure if he was relieved or disappointed that they hadn't all been killed. The look on his lover's face showed that he was feeling the latter; having been the first person to witness their crimes, Keith wanted blood.

Two hours later, the Virginia Port was swamped with FBI and CIA agents. With the scene secure, Dominic and his team were left to police their brass and meet up with the others. Dominic couldn't help but notice the tension radiating off Keith as he quickly stowed his gear and headed towards the van.

Rushing to catch up, Dominic was relieved when Steven agreed to cover the SITREP so he could go check on Keith. Dominic hopped off the container and headed towards the team's van, but when he turned the corner he noticed Keith and Natasha whispering privately.

Unsure if he should intrude, Dominic made sure his approach was heard. Keith and Natasha turned towards him and the look in their eyes said that he was definitely not welcome. It came as a bit of a surprise, but it was Keith's glare that made his steps falter.

"Jesus Christ, he's worse than a fucking puppy. Can't you have five fucking minutes without him chasing you down?" Natasha sneered as she turned her back on Dominic.

Stunned, Dominic turned on his heels and headed back the way he came from; he was not going to take her shit. Yes, the mission was a total goat-fuck, but he had nothing to do with it. Dominic sensed that something about this mission was riding her. Yes, Natasha was always hard to read and sometimes abrupt, but that outburst was extreme even for her.

Fuck it. By the time he made it back to Steven, the rest of their makeshift team had assembled and Lucky was making transport arrangements for the prisoners. They were going to be flown to an unknown facility for questioning.

They were headed back to the airfield to wait for a new ride home.

As Steven and Dominic made their way back to the vehicles, he noticed that Natasha and Keith still stood where he had left them. But instead of huddling together, there seemed to be a new level of tension. Natasha nearly vibrated with anger and Keith seemed ready to explode; whatever had happened in his absence seemed to have gone from bad to combustible.

Keith

"What the fuck was that, Natasha? What the hell is your fucking problem?" Keith roared after he regained the ability to speak. Dominic was already gone, and Keith had little doubt that Natasha was lashing out because this mission was opening barely-healed wounds.

"My problem? Are you fucking kidding me? You popped his cherry. So fucking what? Does he really need to follow you around like the sun rises and sets in your ass? You aren't tired of it yet?" Natasha questioned.

"You have some serious issues, Natasha, and you need to figure this shit the fuck out. I love you; you are my sister. But I am in love with that man, and you will treat him with respect."

"In love? Keith, have you lost your fucking mind? You barely know this guy. You've known me forever. We are family."

Keith's eyes softened as he pulled her into a hug. "Yes, we are family, Natasha, and I love you. But don't make me choose between you," he said. Pressing a kiss to her cheek, he whispered, "Don't make me choose, bol'shaya Sestra, because it will not turn out the way you think."

Keith made his way over to one of the other vehicles. It was obvious that they needed to talk. Natasha was way out of line, but this was something they would need to address in private. He was silent the entire ride, trying to come up with a way to explain what had happened without breaking Natasha's confidence.

As soon as they stopped at the airfield, Keith went to search for Dominic. That whole scene at the docks had been a fuckup and a half. As soon as he had seen Dominic's approach, he had wanted to wave him off.

His mood had been completely volatile, and with Natasha drifting back to her childhood he knew she wouldn't want Dominic to see her so vulnerable. Before he could figure out what to say, though, Natasha had opened her mouth and—as usual—lashed out.

Keith had been so surprised by the pure nastiness and hatred of her words that it had left him totally speechless. By the time his brain had caught up and went to intervene, the damage had been done. The look in Dominic's eyes as he'd caught his gaze had been one hundred percent ice. All the work Keith had done to break down those walls had fallen apart with one look.

Keith understood that he would have some serious apologizing to do, but when Dominic refused to ride with him, opting instead to travel with Stephen, it stung. Of course, his rational mind realized that Natasha was in the vehicle and that was most likely part of the reason. But honestly, he knew he was the other part.

Pissed and annoyed with himself and the entire situation, Keith was determined to fix this fuckup before the situation could deteriorate any further.

Dominic

Not that he'd easily admit it, but Dominic feared rejection and betrayal more than anything. Keith knew this, but he had effectively done both with his earlier actions and silence at Natasha's outburst.

They had approximately three hours before the next plane would arrive. Dominic just wanted to find someplace quiet where he could be alone and relax.

You mean hide from Keith, right? his Angel meddled.

God, I wish I could turn you off sometimes.

Well, you are the one who spends so much time talking to yourself, his Angel shot back. Dominic shook his head and huffed at his own musings.

Finding a secluded spot behind some shipping containers, Dominic stretched out, using his duffle bag as a makeshift pillow. He had almost drifted off into a fitful sleep when a heavy boot kicked his leg.

"What the fuck is your problem, Keith?" He glared up at Keith as the man slid down to take a seat next to him.

"Well, hello to you too, handsome." Keith flashed a wary smile.

Dominic's heart fluttered. Damn, he was falling hard for this man. Just as quick as that thought registered, so did the grim reminder of just how unaffected the man apparently was by him. He frowned at his own weakness. He was letting too much of himself get invested in this relationship.

Chapter 9

Dominic

"Look, Dominic, I'm sorry about earlier. What Natasha said…" Keith sounded flustered, like he couldn't think of the right words. "Not just what she said. What I said. What I didn't say," he rambled.

Suddenly, Dominic needed to move to work out the sudden coil of fear rising in his chest. "Don't worry about it," Dominic cut in.

He was sure whatever Keith was about to say would most likely be some lie to salvage whatever was between them. Dominic didn't want to stomach it; he had done this dance many times over the years when the women he'd dated had called him out on his lack of affection.

"No. Don't do that. Whatever you're thinking right now, just stop. I know this is not coming out right, but fuck, man. I swear I'm not bullshitting you."

Dominic wanted to believe him, everything about his demeanor screamed that he was telling the truth. But fuck it all. The man was a spook; he was a professional liar, trained to beat any type of detection.

"I know you have a million reasons not to trust me right now, but, Dominic, I have never lied to you, and I would never betray your trust. You have to know this by now."

Dominic didn't care how his words made him sound, Keith had become vital to his existence and he had to know for sure that this wasn't a one-sided relationship. "I trust you, Keith, but I have to say I was a bit thrown today. By you. By Shock. But mostly it was your lack of… anything. That fucking hurt. I know she is your friend, and she is obviously hurting, but I thought I meant something to you."

When Keith winced, Dominic knew for certain that he was right to trust that Keith did feel something for him. But all this passive-aggressive bullshit from Natasha was not something he was going to just deal with. Either Keith was going to put a stop to it or he was.

Keith

Keith sat down so his lover could see his eyes as he tried to explain what had happened. "Babe, I can't tell you any details about Natasha. That's her story to tell. But I can tell you that this, this case, hit a nerve for her and that is why she lashed out at you…"

Keith grabbed Dominic's arm when he made to interject.

"Not that she had any right to, which I told her after you left. I was just so shocked at what she was saying that I couldn't speak. She is my best friend, Dominic, and she knows how much I care about you. So I was surprised that she would make it seem like I would have to choose. Because she knows if there is a choice to make, it will be you."

Keith dragged in a breath. He had to get it all out on the table.

"Earlier I was just numb," he continued, afraid that if he didn't lay out all the facts that this might be it. "Between finding those girls and knowing what had been done to them, I just lost it. The scene was just horrific.

Even if I live a hundred years, I will never forget those girls' faces."

He couldn't lose Dominic, not from his own stupidity and not from Natasha's. He would hate to lose Natasha as a friend, but he needed Dominic more. He had never pleaded for someone to forgive him, but now he was completely in love. He would beg if that was what it came down to.

All the fear and anger that had been riding Keith slowly drained away, and he hoped that Dominic could believe all the things he was and wasn't saying. This was something that he understood all too well, how witnessing vicious crimes could consume a man, haunt him.

He knew Dominic still saw the faces of the men he had killed, but the faces of those villagers were the ones that haunted his dreams.

"All right," Dominic answered as he grabbed Keith's hand. "I'm not going anywhere. Do you want to talk about the girls?" Keith's face blanched, and he shuddered at the question. He could see that the man was on the edge and trying to control his emotions, searching for a way to not fall apart.

"Babe, we'll get through this. What do you need?" Dominic asked, changing tactics. Keith's grip tightened for a moment as he closed his eyes to try to get ahold of himself. When he opened them, he knew Dominic would be able to see the naked need burning in his eyes.

"I need you," Keith bit out, his voice rough and demanding. "I need you right here, right now."

Jumping to his feet, Keith reached down to help Dominic to stand. As soon as he was in reach, Keith sealed their mouths together as he turned Dominic to lean against the container. "I want you to use me," he said before dropping to his knees.

Dominic's hand gripping his arm stilled him. "Keith, we don't have to do this," Dominic stated.

"Babe, I want to. I need you," Keith murmured as he resumed their kiss. Dominic pulled back suddenly, and Keith stared at him. "Do you not want to do this?" he asked, suddenly uncertain.

"God, yes, I want to. I want you. I just don't want you to do this because I was pissed at you," Dominic confessed. "I don't want you to have any regrets or feel you have to do anything to make me stay. I want to stay with you. I need you." He leaned forward to swipe their lips together.

As the kiss went on, the intensity increased until it was an all-out explosion of all the emotions twirling in Keith's head. Apparently Dominic was on board as he slid his hands into Keith's hair and anchored in. Dominic shivered and moaned as Keith shoved him hard against the wall.

"I want you here, now," Keith demanded as his hands slid down Dominic's sides. Tracing around his hips, Keith's fingers fumbled briefly before undoing Dominic's belt and pants. He deftly slipped his hand inside to grip the engorged shaft that had already begun leaking copious amounts of fluid.

Keith used his mouth and hands to set a brutal pace. He didn't want to think about the things he had seen earlier. He just wanted to replace those thoughts with the taste of Dominic's cock. He knew they didn't have long before someone came looking for them, but, judging by Dominic's erratic jerks, it wouldn't take much more to push him over the edge.

Dominic

Tell him you love him, his Angel whispered.

Dominic's vision blurred as Keith pumped him with purpose, his wrist twisting on every upstroke. As Keith pushed his thumb into the slit, reasons why this was a bad idea escaped him. He had a moment of clarity as Keith dropped to his knees; off in the distance, he could hear his teammates. But before he could utter a word, Keith swallowed his cock to the root.

Dominic looked down in time to see Keith free his own straining erection. Keith paused to spit on his hand to ease the way before he took Dominic down to the back of his throat, the sound of his mouth slurping and sucking was obscenely loud in Dominic's ears.

Feeling that familiar pull in his balls, Dominic gave up trying to hold off and fisted his hands tightly in Keith's hair. Once he had Keith immobilized, he slammed his cock in as far as he could go and reveled in the gagging sounds.

Dominic pulled back and shoved back in once, twice, and a third time until he had to bite his cheek to stifle his scream. Dominic tasted blood as he dumped what felt like gallons of cum down Keith's throat. Keith moaned his own release as he swallowed convulsively.

Dominic leaned heavily against the container, not yet convinced his legs could support his weight; they felt like overcooked spaghetti. Keith pulled back on his heels, his own hands trembling as he gently tucked in his now flaccid cock before he righted his clothes.

"Hey, babe, we need to get back and see if the plane is ready." Keith's voice helped bring Dominic out of his post-orgasmic haze. Yeah, they really should head back and see if there was anything they could do to get wheels up.

They made themselves as presentable as possible and stumbled back to the group; everyone was busy loading the plane so they were able to slip in with little notice. Dominic could feel Natasha watching him from time to time, but she gave both him and Keith a wide berth, never saying a word.

After the plane ride back, Dominic wanted to just curl up in his bed and forget that the incredibly shitty day had ever happened, but they had to be at the debriefing in one hour. Keith had been quiet since they arrived back at the Hive, and while it wasn't the tense quiet that had sparked their earlier confrontation, something was definitely going on.

"Hey, I'm going to get cleaned up," Keith whispered as soon as they got to his door. Before Dominic could suggest joining him, Keith gave him a quick peck on the lips and disappeared into his room. Apparently he was going alone.

What the fuck was that about?

Dominic had no idea what to make of the sudden change of mood, but rather than go off the handle again, Dominic decided to take a shower himself. He needed time to wrap his head around all the shit that had happened in the last few hours.

The team met up in the conference area to do their after-action reports, and everyone on the team expressed similar concerns about how the targets seemed to have had advance warning of the attack. An uneasy consensus was beginning to form that someone had leaked the information. The conversation quickly escalated to an argument between the team and the FBI and CIA analysts.

No one was going to accept that the leak might have come from their area. Most of the members had been part of their teams for years, so to suddenly call into question their loyalty was worse than a physical blow.

The only new member to join the Hive in the last two years was Dominic, and he couldn't help but feel like he was under scrutiny. Sledge had transferred to the team but had been in one of the other teams for two years so his loyalty was not going to come under question.

Although no one outright accused him, they were no doubt thinking it; he knew he would be thinking the same if he was in their position. Even though Dominic knew he was completely innocent, it did nothing to appease the unease that built in his gut as the meeting came to an unresolved close.

Keith

The entire team headed back towards the living area. Keith had noticed that during the briefing, Dominic had started to withdraw into his brooding mind. No doubt Dominic was somehow taking every negative comment made about a potential leak and turning it into a personal attack.

Keith now knew that he'd definitely made the right plans for the evening. They both had taken more hits to their pride than any one person should stomach for one day. Not to mention the unintentional swipe Natasha had taken towards their relationship.

"Come on, baby, let's go to bed," Keith purred as he guided his dejected boyfriend back towards their room.

Dominic had all but moved into his room, and while it was not official, Keith liked to think of it as their shared space. Keith knew that the meeting had initiated a bad mood, but he knew how to coax his lover back. Dominic had been confused when Keith told him he was showering alone, but for his plan to be effective, it called for this to be a surprise.

They had talked a few times about Dominic topping, and while he was interested, Keith was nervous. They had recently submitted to blood tests, wanting to forgo the condoms, but still Dominic's fear had stopped him from claiming what was his.

No, he never said the words, but Keith knew that his inexperience was what was stalling the action. Keith was never one to sit around and wait for what he wanted, so he had decided to take matters into his own hands.

Dominic was shocked when Keith was all over him as soon as the door closed. "Fuck, baby. What's gotten into you?" he asked between kisses as Keith practically ripped his clothes off.

"Naked... Now..." Keith said in nearly a growl as he yanked Dominic's shirt off and tossed the fabric across the room.

"Shit," Dominic muttered as he reached for Keith's pants, trying to help.

After a few minutes of stumbling and frantic kisses, they were in front of the bed and Dominic had Keith gloriously naked. Dominic slid his hands down Keith's sides, and when he palmed his lover's tight muscular ass and grabbed both cheeks, Dominic startled when his hand hit something hard.

"Babe? What is…" Dominic started.

"It's a plug. I want you to fuck me, Dominic." Keith hissed when Dominic's probing hand caused the plug to shift and nudge his prostate.

Dominic

"Oh God… is that what you were doing in the shower?" Dominic groaned, his voice pained. Keith spun and draped himself over the bed, his thighs spread so his newly-plugged ass was on display.

"Yes, baby… please… I need this." Keith's words turned into a moan as Dominic reached out and grabbed the plug. Toying with it, Dominic found that he enjoyed the way Keith's body bowed as he shifted the toy inside him.

"You like that, baby?" Dominic asked as he slowly twirled the base.

Keith's guttural moan was the only reply.

Dominic pulled the plug slightly out until just the tip remained in that puckered hole before sinking it back inside. Dominic watched in utter amazement as those muscles worked to suck it back inside.

He reached over with his free hand to grab the lube and condoms from under the pillow where they'd taken to stashing them. God, he couldn't wait to feel Keith's ass wrapped around him.

He was so happy they had decided to get tested, but if he had any hope of lasting more than a second, he needed the barrier this first time. Keith growled in displeasure when Dominic released the toy to roll on the condom.

"Shhh… it's okay, baby. I got you. I'm just getting ready," Dominic soothed as he rolled on the condom and damn near drowned his cock in lube. Dominic was rewarded with a sharp gasp as he quickly pulled out the plug.

"You ready, Keith?" Dominic asked, his voice rough as he gently trailed his hand down Keith's side and tried to relax the man beneath him.

Dominic had to firmly squeeze the base of his dick in his free hand, as he teased Keith's slick entrance with his fingers. Dominic pushed ever so slightly against that tight ring, just to feel the resistance; he was tight enough that Dominic was a little afraid to shove his dick in there.

Keith

Keith took a deep breath and let it out slowly, clearing his mind as he forced his body to relax. He wasn't hesitant to be with Dominic this way, but it had been a long, long time since he had been in the receiving position. He took in another deep breath right before Dominic unexpectedly thrust in.

"Shit! Fuck!" Keith screamed, as he clawed at the bedding, trying to anchor himself from the force of Dominic's teeth-clenching penetration.

His entire body throbbed as his ass clenched around Dominic's impressive girth. Dominic stilled but gave him nowhere to run, not with the way he kept his hand firmly between Keith's shoulder blades and held, holding him securely against the bed.

"Oh my God, you are so damn tight. Are you all right?" Dominic's body begged him to move, to do something, but first he had to be sure his partner was ready. As Keith wiggled ever so slightly, sinking him deeper in that vise-like heat, Dominic continued to stroke Keith's back as he trembled.

"Yeah, just give me a sec." Keith panted, as he tried to focus on relaxing his muscles, but, fuck, the man's cock was as thick as his wrist. He couldn't hold in his whimper as he shifted his hips, that thickness rubbing and stimulating areas that had never been touched.

Dominic

"Okay, just tell me when I can move," Dominic rasped. "God, baby, you feel so good." He massaged Keith's lower back and caressed his spine hoping to help him relax and ease the ache. But fuck, he needed to move; every muscle in his body vibrated with need.

Just when Dominic thought his dick was going to explode, Keith whispered, "Okay, I'm ready."

Dominic's caress turned into a tight grip when Keith raised his ass ever so slightly, his balls drawing up tight. Dominic bit his lip hard enough to draw blood, he pulled his cock out until just the tip remained inside. Keith bucked against being held, trying to push himself back. Dominic felt those muscles clench and grasp at his cock as he shoved himself back in.

"Dominic!" Keith yelled out as Dominic set a demanding pace. He dropped his shoulders and cried out nonsense as Dominic braced his hands beside his head and canted his hips in an angle that brushed his gland on every other stroke. The combination of the new leverage and angle had Keith's balls pulling up and his dick leaked furiously.

"Shit… Baby… I'm getting close," Dominic panted. He wanted to hold out until Keith came, but the way his ass was milking Dominic's dick made him feel the urge to come with every stroke. Dominic rose to his knees and pushed Keith's legs farther apart to gain more leverage to pound into him harder.

Within seconds, that wasn't enough; he needed to be deeper, to fuck harder. Tightening his grip until Keith would wear bruises, Dominic began to pull that ass into each thrust. Keith's wails grew louder as Dominic increased the force of his strokes and he quickened his pace.

"Oh, God… Dominic… Fuck… Me… God. Yes!" Keith chanted as each word was accompanied by a forceful slam of Dominic's hips.

"Come on, come for me," Dominic said as he picked up the pace. "You… Are… Mine!" Dominic bellowed as he pounded harder, deeper, faster.

He knew he was done for, but he was determined to drag Keith over with him. Slamming in to the hilt with bone jarring force, Dominic held and ground against Keith's ass as he spilt into the condom.

Keith

The act was primitive, claiming, and all-consuming; Dominic was trying to merge them into one being. Keith knew that he had never been fucked with as much passion or force. It was as if Dominic had put everything he had into their lovemaking.

"Yours... Yours... Yours..." Keith chanted as Dominic demanded that his body follow his commands.

These were orders he had no desire to disobey. His spine arched, and with the final thrust, he shouted into the bed as his body shook violently. His ass clenched down tight and milked his lover, and he shot his load so hard that the first spurt landed on his chin.

Keith went limp, not even attempting to avoid the wet spot. Dazed and exhausted, he couldn't even be bothered with a shower. He heard Dominic move and head toward the bathroom, but he couldn't even muster enough energy to leer at Dominic's nudity as he passed. His body ached pleasantly, and he knew he would have marks where Dominic had gripped him. Yes, he would see and feel the evidence of that fucking for days.

Few words were spoken, but none were needed—they had come together in a way that left little doubt about how they felt for one another. Even with all the drama that had unfolded on the dock, Keith knew with certainty that he would do whatever it took to keep this man at his side.

As much as the thought pained him, Keith silently vowed that he would walk away from Natasha if she continued to poison everything she touched. Keith immediately made contact with Dominic; he shifted and sighed as Dominic took a deep breath and pulled him in tight.

Catching the faintest hint of Dominic's scent mixed in with that of their combined lust, he relaxed into the warmth and comfort of the big man wrapped around him. Keith closed his eyes and inhaled. Enjoying the scent of their lovemaking, Keith smiled, letting that reminder lull him into sleep.

Dominic

Dominic came back into the room with warm rags, and he had to chuckle as he looked at his lover fast asleep. He began the unpleasant task of manipulating the uncooperative man and cleaned him as carefully as possible.

After doing as good of a job as anyone could with an unresponsive subject, he shifted his sleeping lover to make room on the bed. Dominic tossed the rags on the floor—he'd grab those tomorrow—turned off the lights, and climbed into the bed.

Chapter 10

Dominic awoke early to find he was once again completely wrapped around Keith, nose tucked into the crook of his neck. Dominic pulled back and stared at the beautiful man who had spent the last eight months filling him with a lifetime of memories. He watched Keith's slightly curled lips as he continued to sleep.

Getting to this point hadn't been easy. They'd had their share of issues and arguments, but never once did Keith hesitate to show everyone how much he loved Dominic. He never spoke the words, but Dominic saw it in his eyes, tasted it in his kiss, and felt it in his touch; everything he did seemed to stake his claim.

Dominic had never spent any time considering what his life was missing. When he'd been alone, he had always believed that those things were for other men—better men who could offer their partners more than a lifetime of killing. He chose not to want things he couldn't have. Now he had someone who offered him everything, and he saw what he could have every time he looked into Keith's eyes. Just like now.

Keith

Keith sensed he was being watched. As he slowly opened his eyes, he was gifted with the beautiful sight of Dominic watching him carefully. The slow smile that spread across Dominic's face was something Keith looked forward to seeing for a long time.

"Good morning, baby," Keith said as he stretched out.

Still wearing that beautiful smile, Dominic proceeded to shock the shit out of him.

"I love you."

Keith had to blink a few times to make sure he was actually awake. The shock must have shown on his face because Dominic immediately said, "You don't have to say it back. I just wanted you to know. I…"

Keith kissed away whatever Dominic was about to say. He had wanted to say those exact words at least a hundred times over the last few months, but it had never seemed like the right time. He had also feared scaring Dominic off with rushed declarations; he wanted forever with this man, and he was willing to wait as long as it took to get it.

Tracing Dominic's stubble-covered face with his thumb, Keith attempted to pour everything he felt in that kiss. After a few minutes of the sweetest, gentlest kiss they had ever shared, Keith pulled back and whispered, "I love you too, baby."

Keith stared at the face that had become vital to his very existence. Everything in his life paled in comparison to this perfect moment. He reconnected their mouths as he slid his hand down Dominic's chest until he could cup his cock. The man was already hard; his impressive bulge throbbed in Keith's hands.

They fell back to the mattress, and the kiss broke as Keith shifted to hover above Dominic, who stared up at him with a look full of lust and love. Keith nudged Dominic's legs further apart to settle in between, cock to cock. Dominic shuddered as Keith rubbed their erections against one another.

This was all Keith had ever wanted, but he'd never thought he'd have it—the moment he would make love to a man that loved him as much as he returned that love. He smiled down at Dominic, and Keith whispered, "I want you."

"You have me. I belong to you, with you," Dominic said as he stared him unflinchingly in the eyes before he captured Keith's lips.

Dominic

This kiss was not gentle. Keith took control—his tongue stabbing inside, possessive and dominating, a promise of what was to come. Dominic opened to him and moaned his welcome. Keith braced his weight on his elbow and wove his fingers into Dominic's hair, fisting it tight and using it to drag his man closer as he turned up the heat.

Dominic ran his hands up Keith's back; not wanting him to get away, he arched his back to maximize their points of contact. As Dominic's fingertips dug deeper into Keith's muscular shoulders, Keith deepened the kiss, but Dominic still needed more.

When the need for oxygen became vital, Keith pulled back, gulping air before he ducked his head and found Dominic's nipple and sucked. Dominic bucked and thrashed as Keith chewed on one then the other. Dominic's blunt nails scored down Keith's back as he bowed up and pushed his nipple deeper in Keith's mouth.

Dominic reached behind him, his hand searching for their supplies under the pillow; coordination was a foreign concept as Keith bit down on his nipple hard enough to hurt. He whimpered in relief as his hand wrapped around the lube and a condom. He moaned wantonly as his other nipple was subjected to the same torture.

"Baby, I want to be with you bare," Keith said when Dominic handed him the lube and condom. Without a second thought, Dominic grabbed the condom and tossed it to the floor. They had constant health screenings, and they'd each had a complete STD screening over a month before.

Dominic had simply been waiting for Keith to say he was ready. There was no doubt in his mind that this was the man he would be with for the rest of his life.

Dominic could only manage a shaky, "Yes," as the *snick* of the bottle opening drowned out his gasping groans. His hole twitched in anticipation.

Never would have pegged us as an eager bottom, his Angel confessed. But even his inner monologue seemed to be put on hold as he thrust his hips up blindly, seeking to speed up the process.

Keith

"Okay, just take it easy, baby," Keith murmured as he kneed Dominic's legs further apart. He grasped behind Dominic's knees and pushed them up toward his chest. "Just relax, baby, I've got you," he said as his slippery fingers slid between his lover's cheeks.

Keith teased and petted Dominic's entrance; he enjoyed the keening moans Dominic gave up as he pushed a digit inside. Dominic groaned as he pushed in, pumping that finger for only a few seconds before he quickly added a second.

Dominic had taken beautifully to bottoming and although Keith had no problem letting him take the lead, the fact that Dominic trusted him to go where no one ever had before made topping him the most exquisite experience.

Keith tore a gasp from Dominic's throat when he crooked his fingers and bumped Dominic's gland. Keith licked a nipple and repeated the move; Dominic shook and clenched his ass around that intrusion.

"There it is, God! I love watching you," Keith said. He blew across Dominic's wet nipple, pulled tight from the constant stimulation.

"Keith… Please… I'm so close. I need you to fuck me now." He groaned as Keith tapped his prostate again and again.

He was strung tight and barely held on. If Keith kept rubbing his prostate, he was going to come soon, with or without him.

Keith

Keith sat up, grabbed the lube, and liberally applied it to his cock to ensure a smooth fucking. Keith gripped his cock in one hand and used the other to separate Dominic's cheeks to better see his target. Dominic pushed back as he pressed against that still-oh-so-tight rosette, and they both let out a moan when Keith pushed into that heat.

Keith kept pressing in. He whispered words of encouragement until he was halfway in and stilled. Keith leaned forward and kissed Dominic, swallowing each of his moans, as his hips began to pump.

Keith felt himself slide deeper on every press forward. Even though his progression was constant, he remained gentle. Dominic was still much too tight to rush. Once his hips were pressed firmly against Dominic's ass, he held still and allowed Dominic enough time to adjust to Keith's girth and length.

Keith sucked on Dominic's bottom lip and slid his tongue inside as he waited for his lover to accommodate him. No matter how many times they did this, Keith was never willing to hurt this man that trusted him so completely.

He couldn't, however, stop his body from trembling as Dominic's ass quivered around him. Keith focused on Dominic's face and waited for the moment it relaxed completely so he could finally give in to his need to grind.

"Fuck, Keith, I need you to move." Dominic lifted his hips and squeezed around Keith's length to punctuate his desire.

Keith moaned and rotated while grinding down, stimulating that sensitive tissue and nudged Dominic's gland.

"Jesus Christ, just fuck me, Keith, like you know you want to." Dominic moaned in frustration when Keith refused to speed up the pace.

Keith was determined to memorize every inch of Dominic. He wanted to push in so deep that they ceased to exist outside of each other. Keith pulled back slowly until only the tip of his cock remained squeezed in those tight muscles.

"No, baby, I don't want to fuck you…" He pushed in just as slowly, then slammed in hard the last few inches and stilled again, making sure to rub against Dominic's prostate.

Dominic

Dominic wailed as Keith hit that spot that made his balls ache. He grabbed the sheets beside his hips and arched his back, trying to get Keith to move again.

"I am a very selfish man," Keith warned as he rotated his hips to massage Dominic's prostate. "I want to carve out a place inside you." He repeated the move: slow retreat with a slow press inside and a snap of his hips at the last second so he hit Dominic's prostate straight on.

Dominic groaned and cried out unintelligible words as his body was wracked with spasms.

"A place only I can fill," Keith finished as he rubbed and ground on that spot that curled Dominic's toes and arched his back off the bed.

Dominic wanted to tell Keith that he already had all those things and more, but he was completely incapable of speech. Wave after wave of intense pleasure shattered his mind and reduced him to begging moans and gasps.

Dominic dropped his legs from Keith's shoulders and draped them over his arms, raising his hips to encourage the wicked strokes to his gland. Keith didn't disappoint, adjusting his angle so he hit the mark on every pump. "Just…like…that… Right there… Jesus… Fuck, Keith!" Dominic roared, each word stuttered to match the stroke of Keith's cock to his highly-sensitive gland.

Rough hands gripped Dominic's hips, helping to tilt his body into the position Keith wanted. He slowly pulled back. Keith moaned, obviously enjoying his new leverage. "Fuck," Dominic cursed as those slow, deep thrusts made his engorged cock leak and flush a deep angry red.

Suddenly, Keith pulled Dominic onto his cock as he slammed forward. Dominic nearly screamed on impact, and his hands scrambled for purchase gripping the sheets. Keith savagely snapped his hips; he continuously tugged Dominic down and onto his cock. "Fuck! Fuck! Fuck! Fuck!" Dominic's passion-filled profanity accompanied each back-breaking stroke.

In all their times together, Keith had never taken him with such utter abandon; gone was the careful lover who guided him to ecstasy, replaced by a rutting beast determined to squeeze every ounce out of this sinful pleasure. Dominic reveled in the debauchery of being so thoroughly used.

"Do you like that?" Keith snarled.

"Yes. God, yes." Dominic's enthusiastic reply stuttered as Keith pressed their bodies together tightly, grinding his hips so his dick massaged Dominic's prostate.

"Can you come this way?" Keith murmured. "Just from me fucking you?" He jerked his hips back an inch only to slam home again.

"Oh, God... Keith! I don't know." Dominic knew he could; in fact, he felt his orgasm swirling, itching up his spine, but the edge remained just outside his reach.

Keith changed his pace, fast then slow, hard and grinding, and Dominic couldn't keep up. His chest heaved with each desperate attempt to inhale enough air to keep from passing out.

"Fuck, please..." Dominic whimpered—and shuddered as more frustrated sounds slipped from his throat.

Dominic pulled in a deep breath as his shoulders tensed and trembled. He honestly didn't know if he could get off just from the delicious feeling in his ass, but he was afraid to let go of the sheets to stroke himself. He didn't want to move in case the angle changed. No, he wouldn't do anything to throw off Keith's earth-shattering tempo.

Dominic dug his nails into Keith's sides where his hands had slid at some point. No doubt he was breaking skin, but he couldn't force any of his muscles to relax as Keith dragged out an orgasm so fierce his vision darkened and he thought he might actually faint.

He opened his mouth in a silent scream as his stomach clenched and endless pulses of spunk shot out, milking his balls painfully. He vaguely registered Keith slamming into him and freezing before scalding heat flooded his passage. His balls tightened again and forced a pitiful dribble of cum to seep in response.

Keith

Keith was pretty sure that Dominic was primed to come hands-free and he was determined to give him that game-changing orgasm. He gripped Dominic's hips hard and slammed in to the hilt; Keith kept the pressure on his prostate. He could feel Dominic's muscles tighten around his cock, the grip just this side of painful.

Dominic screamed profanities and nonsense as Keith fucked him at a pace that was sure to tip Keith over, but not before the man beneath him fell apart. Dominic's startled shriek held surprise and pleasure, and his arms wrapped around Keith as Dominic tried in vain to pull him closer.

Keith knew he didn't have much longer. As he fought back his own need to climax, he widened his stance and aimed his hips so his cock would make direct contact with Dominic's prostate. He knew he hit his mark when the man in question babbled syllables and those tight muscles contracted further, painfully.

Chapter 11

The tension in the group was so thick it was like a living thing. Everyone sensed that there was more than just bad luck playing out in the last two missions. There was no proof, but somehow their missions were compromised. How had each mark known they were being targeted?

No one ever had a perfect mission; no matter how well they planned, no matter how much they trained, the human element was always unpredictable. This was one constant fact of any mission, the reason why they trained relentlessly: to be prepared for any and all eventualities. But there was something about these last two missions that just reeked of deception.

With both being marginally successful and this new mission coming so quick on the heels of the last, the potential for things to go seriously sideways was too great to be ignored.

Intel had come in that a terrorist cell was using a garage to recruit suicide bombers and had a warehouse with drugs and weapons set for shipment. There was no telling how many attacks that sale would fund.

So, with a little less than one week's notice, all three teams were to conduct an all-out assault with spotty confirmation and an unknown number of combatants. Normally, they gathered months of required intelligence before a plan was laid out, but this was too big to wait. That this terrorist cell had supposedly been operating in their back yard without detection made the mission reek of some sort of trap.

Lucky contacted Washington with his concerns, but without any hard proof, there was no way the CIA was going to let this go. So they settled into the case and tried to piece together the raid. Even as each new piece fit together perfectly—too perfectly—they had a mission to complete.

Not only did they need to shut down the operation, but they also needed to capture and detain the ring leaders. The team had information on the terrorists setting up shop in Atlanta but needed to know who was funding it.

Headquarters seemed to take the mission as a simple task that could yield a body of information, but as the actual bodies started to pile up, it became clear that somehow their prey was wise to their approach.

Dominic and Steven set up their positions. There were eight snipers, four more than they originally planned, but teams two and three decided to bring in their own snipers as well, as their team captains voiced their concerns with the mission.

They were set to take out the combatants that tried to escape, as well as contain any attempts of reinforcements. As Dominic peered through his night-vision goggles, everything seemed off, and strAngely, the stillness made his hackles rise as he continued to search the perimeter.

Dominic set up his sniper's nest on the far side of the perimeter. Steven radioed that the foot traffic easily doubled what they had hoped for. He radioed the other snipers and the ground teams about the situation. They worked quickly to revise their strategy of attack, opting to move in from the north where the side entrance was located.

Samuel

Sam checked his vest and clips and secured his suppressor as they moved in darkness, careful to avoid being seen in the moonlight. They headed for the auto repair shop being used as a recruitment station for would-be terrorists. Chaos had radioed that there were at least four men outside the doors. Sledge and Lucky moved up silently and made contact almost immediately.

"Contact," Sam reported as he dropped his first target, a small report sounding as the man crumpled quickly. He sidestepped to engage the second guard; Sam put two rounds in the combatant's chest before he could lift his weapon in response.

Lucky

The final two guards stood off to the corner. Lucky dropped to a knee as they turned in response to Sam's assault. He aimed in. His shots were quiet; the first man never saw it coming, and when the second target sprayed bullets—they grazed the post Lucky knelt behind—he squeezed the trigger and hit the final man in the stomach.

"We've been made," Lucky advised as he scanned the area.

Six armed gunmen sprinted from the garage, lights shining to pick out the team's positions. Apparently they had lost the element of surprise long before the first shot rang out. These men were heavily armed, as if they waited for the attack, with automatic machine guns and a large numbers of combatants.

They were not foot soldiers looking to recruit a new suicide bomber.

Dominic

Keith and Natasha raced to their designated areas as rooftop floodlights washed the surrounding area. "Chaos, hit the lights!" Natasha commanded, the added light undoubtedly destroying her night vision.

Natasha stepped out of hiding as she opened fire on the group headed in her direction, abandoning the post she had set up behind.

"I'm on it," Dominic replied as he sighted in on the hand-held search light. Obviously these men had been somehow warned. His round punched through the light and continued through the chest of his target.

"We have a problem. Multiple targets at every door. We could use some assistance," Lucky growled in her earpiece.

After Samuel extinguished his human lantern, Dominic readjusted to provide cover for Lucky and Sam. Their orders to minimize casualties went out the window, and they were forced to follow their own protocols to ensure they achieved their objective. They were to take the target at all cost, but first they had to breach the facility—

and the survival of their ground men was the primary objective.

"Chaos, we need you to clear a path to the side door to secure the target," Keith radioed as they moved up the perimeter.

Now that Dominic and Steven could focus on picking off tangos as they left the building, the ground team would have an easier job securing the area.

"Solid copy," Dominic replied as he began to eliminate the shooters between Keith and the door. The other snipers cleared the path wide enough that the rest of the team was able to move on the offensive and storm the building.

Samuel

As they made their way out of the closed garage bays and toward the back room, a spray of bullets shattered the glass, sending them scattering for cover. A ricocheting bullet struck the sixty-pound air compressor causing a massive explosion in the garage, the force turning the doors into projectiles.

As the hail of bullets breezed past his head, Sam made a dive for cover and was unprepared for the explosion that flung him like a rag doll across the room, slamming him against the concrete wall. His arm snapped as he hit the ground; shrapnel peppered his skin as he attempted to drag himself to safety.

Sam applied a small amount of weight on his injured arm. He choked as smoke began to suck the oxygen from the room. He howled in agony as his vision blurred.

Lucky

"Report!" Lucky bellowed as he groped around for his weapon.

As each member began to give a status report, Lucky noticed two members did not respond. The smoke started to clear as agents took out the windows. Lucky could just make out the sound of someone crying out.

"Lucky, I'm over here."

Lucky ordered the team to continue forward as he sought out the injured. The first agent he came across was dead. He had taken the impact of one of the doors; his upper torso was postured in an unnatural angle.

He almost passed the body partially hidden by the tank and other debris that had flown in. As he approached, he realized that his own man was down. Carefully, Lucky removed the wreckage that blocked his path. He called for Eric when he felt Sam's pulse strong and steady beneath his fingertips.

"Doc, I need a medevac. Sledge is down, unconscious, burns and a possible broken arm. His vitals are steady, but he's unresponsive," Lucky supplied details as he checked for other injuries. Eric responded immediately with a ten-minute ETA. Lucky was about to splint the arm when Natasha stormed into the room.

"Lucky, we need you in the other—" Natasha broke off when she recognized Sam. The color drained from her face as a look of utter panic colored her features, but she slid back into her professional demeanor so smoothly, Lucky almost missed the promise of murder in her eyes.

"We need you in the other room. The target attempted to off himself. They are stabilizing him now. I'll stay with Sledge until we can move him."

There wasn't really time to linger. He quickly gave her the rundown before double timing to see how fucked the situation had become. Lucky radioed the Hive with the latest developments. "All the targets have been eliminated or detained. We have three casualties and two severely injured. We are going to need some birds in the air and a cleanup crew. The local police are here, and we are stalling, but we need a plausible story to go with."

The second team field medic placed an IV in their target. "Self-inflicted gunshot to the chest, small caliber looks like. He missed everything vital but if we want to

keep him alive we need to get him moved and soon," he
said.

"Fuck! I need an estimate on that bird or our target
is going to bleed out," Lucky called back to Command as
he frowned at the shredded documents burning in the
containers. The mission was a total goat-fuck and other
than shutting down the recruitment station, they hadn't
been able to secure one piece of intelligence.

There is no way this is a coincidence. Lucky
surveyed the smashed and burned electronic equipment.
This was the third mission where their targets were
completely aware of the strike, so there had to be a leak
some–fucking–where. He could taste it.

Lucky slammed out of the room to check on the
survivors, vowing to find whoever was fucking over his
team. Natasha knelt, speaking softly to Sam as he was also
having an IV placed. "How is he doing, Doc?" Lucky asked
as he watched Eric work.

"Well, he's been whining as usual, so I am going to
predict he will be fine," Eric answered as he smiled at Sam.

Sam returned his smile with a bitten off, "Fuck you,
Doc." He winced as his damaged arm was splinted.

Dominic

Dominic policed his brass and secured his perch, ensuring there would be no trace of the activities on the rooftops. As he looked out on the scene, he grimaced at the number of bodies that littered the area.

No way was this just a chance encounter, his Angel nagged.

He had heard the radio calls of the number of dead and injured; someone had decided to wage war against the Hive, and they were winning.

Dominic causally strolled towards the group as the first bird touched down. The target was loaded, and they were airborne before he made it across the perimeter.

"The bird for the injured has a three-minute ETA," the pilot radioed down to the team as he cleared the buildings and headed toward some unknown medical facility. Sam cursed vehemently about his clothing being destroyed, and Dominic had to laugh.

Can't be too bad if his T-shirt is his greatest concern, his Angel chuckled.

"Hey, man, maybe you should have stayed with your truck. Since you couldn't avoid getting your ass blown up…" Dominic joked as he gently palmed Sam's head and rested their foreheads together.

"You know me, man. I'd do anything to get out of those early morning PT sessions." Sam snickered. It felt good to joke with the man, reassurance that Sam was indeed alive and well.

Chapter 12

Knowing they'd been set up was a tough enough pill to swallow, but knowing that three Hive members were now dead, and two more were wounded with no idea who was on their six was unacceptable. Add to it that one of the injured was Sledge, and the whole scenario left the team reeling and searching for someone to lash out at.

Whoever pulled the strings had to have some working knowledge of how the Hive worked. They had known exactly how to draw in the entire team. It was not an easy task to hide and fund a large terrorist cell in the best of conditions, but to have such a fortified building go undetected meant this mole went deep in the organization.

Dominic and Steven cleaned their rifles in complete silence; there was nothing to say. Each man went through the motions, on complete autopilot as they reviewed every round they sent downrange. No one had really spoken since they returned to the Hive. They had been given their times to provide their after-action reports and were sent to clean and stow their gear.

Lucky had been eerily mute, not bothering with anything other than what was essential. It was obvious to everyone that their commander was readying himself to wage war to find out who was attempting to blow their cover.

The Hive was packed with CIA agents who were going over every piece of intel of the mission with each team member interviewed individually. It was almost insulting that the prevailing thought was that someone inside the Hive had gone rogue.

But as much as that charge stung, there was no way around the fact that they had somehow known when, where, and how the attack was going to be launched. They obviously hadn't been told about the number of snipers, but that was little in the way of condolences.

Dominic finished cleaning his weapon and checked it into the armory. He needed to get cleaned up before his interview. Hopefully he would have time to visit Sledge before facing the inquisition.

He reached the infirmary and found Natasha standing outside the door; she paced in the corridor, her steps broadcasting her feelings.

Dominic grew concerned when Natasha failed to notice his presence. She was a woman who always noticed everything, but now she seemed lost as she fiddled with the collar she had taken to wearing. She was the picture of a distressed civilian. Her icy demeanor had been completely abandoned. There was more than just a concerned friend; maybe this was her lover...

Hmm, that was something he would have to think about later.

"How is he doing?" Dominic asked. Her startled expression solidified his assessment that she had not sensed his arrival. She looked at him and blinked several times, her eyes red and glassy with unshed tears.

The door opened, breaking their connection before she could respond. Eric came out carrying a bag of what looked to be Sam's tattered clothing.

"The burns were superficial, but his arm was broken. He'll need a cast for the next six weeks but will make a full recovery." Eric looked directly at Natasha as he made his assessment, further suggesting that Natasha and Sam had a deeper connection than just friends.

Natasha walked straight into the room, pausing only to weakly smile at Eric as he patted her shoulder. There was a look that passed between them, and Dominic did a double take. As the door closed, Dominic was sure there was something going on that he wasn't privy to. He paused, unsure if he should intrude.

He figured Natasha would tell Sam he was in the hall. Dominic decided to sneak in now and quickly leave them to… to do whatever.

"Hey, bud, how are you feeling?" Dominic asked. Sam was sitting up, his arm casted and a barrage of bandages covering his naked torso.

Sam replied with a sarcastic smirk, "I feel like someone blew up my truck." He laughed and winced.

Dominic chuckled at his cheeky reply.

After a few minutes of mindless chatter, Dominic excused himself to report for his debriefing. He arrived at the situation room just in time to see Keith leaving it. The look on his face was murderous, and Dominic wondered just what was in store for him.

"Have a seat, Staff Sergeant Muccino," said the one agent who was already seated at the conference table. Dominic took the seat indicated and waited for the questions to start. They sat in silence for a full minute before the second agent took the seat directly across from him.

"SSgt. Muccino, do you know a former SSgt. Sean Harper and a Major Brandon Elliot?" the first agent asked as he spread out printed emails and pushed them across to Dominic for him to read. Dominic's mind raced as he tried to understand how these men that he'd left so long ago could be involved in what had been happening to the team now.

As he read the emails that spelled out each of their failed missions in great detail, Dominic's stomach roiled. His name was mentioned in several emails, including their time spent together in Afghanistan, and they made several mentions of how he was the lone member of their team who had not been jailed.

There were photos of each of his team members, along with detailed descriptions of their jobs and skill sets. Several photos time-lined and documented Keith and his relationship including each time they had ventured out together. It seemed so well documented. There were even photos of them inside the Hive. They spoke of their inside connection to the Hive, and although they never mentioned the person by name, Dominic had no doubt who these agents thought was the leak.

"Where the fuck did you get this?" Dominic roared as he jumped to his feet.

Agent Two slid his hand by his sidearm as he said, "Before the last mission."

Dominic snapped and grabbed Agent One by the throat. "How long, asshole?" he asked even as Agent Two pressed his weapon to Dominic's head. "How long have you known that my team was in danger?" he asked again, oblivious to the threat as he wrapped both hands around his target's throat.

"About a week before this mission," Agent One wheezed around the hand squeezing the life out of him.

Keith and Natasha slammed into the room, but all that did was make Dominic squeeze harder. "Dominic, I need you to stand the fuck down!" Keith barked. "Dominic," Keith growled again, but Dominic was way past the point of caring.

"They knew, Keith. They knew we had a fucking leak, and they sent us in anyway," Dominic bellowed and

Agent One's eyes bulged as he applied more pressure. "So what was it? Did you think I was the leak? Or did you just not give a fuck if my whole team died as long as we completed your mission?" he asked the soon-to-be-dead man that he held.

Lucky

Lucky spoke calmly as he walked up beside Dominic. "Staff Sergeant Muccino, back off. We know you are not the leak, and I will be taking care of these two agents." To the second agent, he said, "Secure your weapon, agent, before you get yourself hurt." The agent looked at him and then back at Dominic, hesitating.

"Agent, I am not going to say it again: secure your weapon. I mean right the fuck now!" Lucky made eye contact to impress upon the man that his life was indeed in danger if he failed to follow Lucky's command again. As the agent holstered his weapon and stepped away, Lucky focused on talking Dominic off the ledge.

"Dominic, it's handled. Let the agent go so I can take care of this." Lucky sighed internally when Dominic obeyed. "Keith, please take Dominic to his quarters until I have the chance to speak with him." Dominic's face was that of a man who had been pushed too far, and Lucky knew they were going to need everyone in top condition for the new game being played.

As Dominic and Keith left the room, Lucky took a seat at the vacated conference table. "So gentlemen, now is where you explain to me what is going on." His smile was feral as he addressed the agents, they looked at one another before they took their seats.

Agent Two offered, "Sir, about a week ago, headquarters was able to decrypt the computers you found aboard the Russian cargo ship. These documents were discovered in the emails, the photos, as well as the information provided to the terrorist group. While we were unable to uncover the name of the leak, we did verify that it came from inside the Hive."

"All right, so what you are telling me is that you knew there was a leak inside the Hive, and you just decided I didn't need to know."

Lucky ground his teeth so hard they ached as he tried to quell the urge to beat the man's head on the table.

"Not only that," Lucky roared, "but you then proceeded to send the entire Hive out on a mission that was compromised at best, and a total setup at worst!"

The two agents scrambled to try and salvage the situation. "No, sir. All conceivable measures were in place to ensure the Hive's safety. At no point was there any intelligence suggesting that the mission was anything other than it appeared." Agent One's voice was raspy from Dominic's hands.

Good.

Lucky jumped from his seat, interrupting whatever they were about to say next. "All conceivable measures?" he asked, his patience at its end. "So you never *conceived* that it might have been a good fucking idea to inform *me* and the other commanders of the risk we were sending our men into?" He fumed, spittle flew from his lips.

"I want to know who made this call. Was Langley informed of this situation?" he asked as the men cowered in their seats.

"Umm… No… No, sir. The field handler felt it was best to keep this as close to the chest as possible. He did not want to get Washington involved. Sir..." Agent Two added as they both realized the shit storm they were in.

"Well, gentlemen, I'm afraid we've found ourselves at an impasse here. Why don't you two sit tight while I contact Washington and see what their take on this situation will be?" Lucky just nodded at Natasha as he went to his office to call headquarters. Though he posed it as a suggestion, Natasha would ensure those agents stayed put until he could get some answers.

Lucky made it halfway through his situation report before his Washington handler exploded. He grinned, even though he knew the man couldn't see him. "Are you fucking kidding me? For all we know, the leak came from the controller's office," his handler said.

"That is my opinion exactly, and the fact that my objections to the mission were ignored and we were sent out unprepared leaves me to lean heavily in that direction," he added, just to make sure his handler had a full idea of how deep this mole might go; the controllers mostly came from high up in Washington.

"Lieutenant Simmons, I am going to need you to handle this as quickly and quietly as possible. The director is giving you full authority to investigate as you see fit. The leak needs to be interrogated and eliminated. We cannot have this come back and blow up in our faces. The President needs to be advised, so I'll be contacting you directly for reports. You and your team will be given letters of blanket immunity; this situation needs to be handled. No one, and I mean no one—other than myself, the director, or the President—is to hear a word of this. Do you understand?"

Lucky smiled wide. "Yes, sir, that is a solid copy," he acknowledged before ending the call. Sitting back in his chair, Lucky let his mind wander as he contemplated the team's next move. Obviously these men had targeted Dominic, and the first order of business was to figure out why.

Lucky strolled back to the two agents in the conference room, not even attempting to hide the contempt he held for them. He addressed his prisoners as soon as he entered the room. "Okay, gentlemen, it seems as if you will be staying here a while longer. Natasha will contact your supervisors and inform them of your need to further investigate. Gentlemen, she will need your phones."

Natasha immediately began to pat them down. He gave a curt nod. There was no way he was leaving these two any opportunity to warn anyone.

Dominic

Keith stayed silent as they slammed out of the conference room. "Dominic, what the hell happened in there?" Keith questioned as he closed them off in Dominic's room. He had not uttered a single word since they left the conference room and Keith knew enough about him to recognize his warning signs.

Dominic took several deep breaths and released them slowly, trying to get ahold of his temper. Just when Keith looked like he was going to ask again, Dominic finally spoke.

"I know who is setting us up." He paused, looked in his lover's eyes, and wondered if Keith would believe that he had no clue what was going on up until a few minutes ago.

"Before I left the military, I was stationed in Afghanistan. I was assigned to a new unit after their sniper was killed when their bird crashed. That is where I met my ex-partner Staff Sergeant Sean Harper and my ex-commander Major Brandon Elliot."

Dominic closed his eyes as the memories flashed in front of him, as if they happened yesterday.

"On our last mission, I was assigned to hit a village where a terrorist was hiding. After taking the target, the ground troops were to storm the village and take out any remaining hostiles. Our orders included questioning the locals on the location of other terror cells while SSgt. Harper and I remained outside to provide cover. After a few rounds of questions, the Major started executing civilians. I tried to intervene and was knocked out."

The faces of the villagers he had failed to protect appeared before him, and he opened his eyes.

Dominic sucked in a breath, determined to finish while he could. "When I woke up, I was in the hospital with a fractured skull and was informed that the mission had been a success and there had been no survivors."

He grimaced as waves of nausea rolled through him, just like they had that day.

"I contacted my old commander and told him what had really happened in those mountains. Long story short, I testified against those assholes. The rest of the team covered for them, claiming they were attacked by insurgents after I was out and were forced to defend themselves. Since I couldn't dispute that claim, SSgt.

Harper and Major Elliot got four years each and a dishonorable while the rest of the unit was disbanded and received shorter brig time. After that, there wasn't anywhere to serve as a snitch, so here I am," Dominic finished and braced himself for his lover's reaction.

"Fuck, babe. We had heard that you had some serious shit go down and that is why your records were sealed, but fuck…" Keith looked at him, and Dominic couldn't be sure what he saw swirling in those blue-gray eyes but Keith's voice begged him to believe. "We'll get these guys, babe."

"That is not the only thing they said. There is more…" Dominic didn't know whether to laugh or cry. Keith honestly wasn't drawing any conclusions on whom it was the CIA seemed to think was their leak.

"Okay…" Keith led, and Dominic knew he wouldn't let go until he said it.

"Me! Fuck, Keith, they think I'm the fucking leak! They found emails that discussed the leak. My name was in those emails, not naming me the leak but establishing my connection to those fuckers. They have fucking pictures—pictures and intelligence on every member of our team.

God knows our cover is blown to shit; who the fuck else got those fucking pictures?"

Dominic paced as his voice rose with every declaration.

"They have pictures of us, Keith; me and you, in and outside the Hive," he whispered.

Through everything, Dominic's greatest fear had been that he would be exposed and involve his lover in his fucked up past. Even if by some small miracle Keith could look past it, he would never forgive himself. Dominic had always taken it as a fact that his life would most likely end violently; it was the way he lived, but to drag someone else in… That was unacceptable.

"Whatever you are thinking right now, stop it. I can tell you without hesitation that no one, not one fucking person in this Hive, will think that you are the leak."

Keith stood directly in front of Dominic to halt his sporadic pacing.

"We know you. I fucking know you, Dominic, and I know you have more integrity than ten men. No one will question your honesty or loyalty," Keith finished as he searched Dominic's face.

Dominic grabbed his wrist. "Keith, I never meant to drag you into this fight. Fuck, I didn't even know there was a fight to drag you into." He let Keith's wrist go to run his shaky hands through his hair.

Keith laughed, although the sound lacked any humor. "Look, I am flattered you are concerned about me, but if you think I am some helpless damsel..." Keith scoffed. "Well, I might just have to kick the shit out of you myself." He palmed Dominic's face to force the man to look at him.

Keith

"Come on. We are both mercenaries for the CIA. Our jobs are not safe. I've got more warrants and contracts out for my life than I've got fingers and toes. So the concept of two ex-Marines with a grudge just doesn't rank high on my give-a-fuck list. We knew going in this was the deal and I accept that. I accept that by being with you, your enemies are now mine," Keith pleaded with him.

He could see that Dominic was thinking of running, and he wouldn't allow him that option. Before they could finish, there was a brief knock on the door right before the commander walked in.

"Keith, Dominic and I need to talk. Go talk to Natasha and she will catch you up on our current situation," Lucky ordered. Keith nodded and squeezed Dominic's shoulder before he left the room without a word and closed the door behind him.

Lucky

"Well, son, I don't need to tell you the seriousness of what is about to go down." Lucky carefully assessed his sniper. He needed to know if Dominic was going to be any good in this battle.

The situation in the ready room had been a peek into what Lucky knew was a volatile temper that was usually well restrained. But this snafu was on a level so epic that Lucky would have been worried if the man hadn't snapped.

"No, sir," Dominic sneered.

"Good, so I shouldn't have to tell you that I have received the green light from command to terminate both marks and ferret out our rat," Lucky continued.

"Sir, I understand that the information was damaging but—"

Lucky interrupted him. "If you are about to ensure me that you are not our leak, I can just stop you right there."

Lucky put a hand up to silence what would no doubt be a damn interjection.

"Dominic, not one fucking person in my command believes for a second that you have anything to do with this clusterfuck. If you think any information from your past might sway my assessment, sorry, kid, I already knew everything."

He raised an eyebrow at Dominic's surprise.

"Fuck, do you really think I don't know about every breath you've drawn since the day you were born? Then you are fucking dumber than I thought."

He chuckled at the man's honest astonishment.

Lucky shook his head as he walked closer to Dominic. "All you need to be doing right now is figuring out how we can fuck these guys. Everything has been handled," he said and gave Dominic's shoulder a squeeze.

Dominic

"What you tell the team is up to you. Your records are sealed, but trust me when I say no one would think any less of you for it." Lucky had reached the door by the time he finished his speech.

As he walked out, Dominic noticed that Keith had not returned. He hedged between being grateful for his absence and wishing for the comfort he knew the man would give. Truth was, Dominic had no idea what the fuck he needed.

Well, that is a fucking lie, his Angel nagged as he sprawled across his mattress.

He needed to figure out how to find those motherfuckers. And when he did, Dominic would finally get to do what he should have done all those years ago— put a bullet in both their heads.

And after that… After that was the biggest mind fuck of them all. The past year had been amazing, and Dominic really felt as if he had found where he needed to be. But now it seemed that his past was not going to stay buried. Maybe in some way he was never supposed to be happy. Now it looked like he would have to move on.

Regardless of what Lucky said, Dominic lived in the real world.

And just like the Marines, once he was put under question, no one would ever trust him again. The thought of yet another family turning their backs on him made Dominic want to hit something. Maybe instead of giving him a second chance, the fates just wanted him to taste how good it could be, just so the pain would be torture when everything was taken away.

Keith. Dominic had known from the beginning that he had never done a thing in his life to deserve Keith. He was everything Dominic could have wanted in a partner and for a little while he had almost believed he could keep it.

Keith had once claimed that he was selfish, but Dominic knew without a doubt that it was him that was greedy.

Because as much as he didn't deserve to be here— and God knew he didn't deserve Keith or to be loved—now that he had tasted it, he wanted it. No, he needed it. He just had to figure out how to keep it.

Chapter 13

The situation was entirely his fault. His demons were coming home to roost and now not only was his life in danger, but his team's lives were as well. Sean and Brandon had gone completely off the fucking reservation, but as crazy as they were, they still had to have someone helping them.

Lucky wanted him to figure out their game and how to put them in the kill box. No matter what angle Dominic approached it with, two crazed Marines couldn't have pulled all this off. It just didn't make sense. There was no way they could have believed that they would live through this suicide mission.

The CIA had limitless power and a blanket of immunity, but launching an attack against their own country to avenge some old grudge? No, there had to be more to the game than what had been presented.

Dominic needed time to think. Since that day in Afghanistan, he had been playing catch-up with these two. How they managed to get a relatively short sentence for such a heinous crime was something that had continuously haunted him. They had to have had someone pretty high on the food chain vouch for them; that was the only thing that made sense.

Now finding out who was pulling the strings was literally a matter of life or death. Even if—or when—they found those two, they would never be taken alive. Dominic knew this as well as he knew his own face. The fact that they had tipped their hand, revealing their identity, proved that they had no intention of surrendering; they would play this game all the way to the end.

Dominic laid in his bed, going back over everything he could remember about the time he served with them. He had been a last-minute addition to the team; the sniper that was assigned to that unit had died when his helicopter went down.

It was no secret that they didn't want him as a replacement, but Dominic had always considered that just a unit showing its loyalty. Those men had been together for years; no new guy was just going to walk in and be accepted.

But now it seemed that there was more to it than what his first glance had shown. Maybe whoever was helping them now had something to do with what happened in that village. That was the one thing Dominic never understood: what would make a career Marine completely flip his shit and start killing villagers?

And was it just a coincidence that they used a terror cell to lure in his hive?

Anything can be a coincidence until it isn't, his helpful Angel offered.

Sometimes getting to the truth was like peeling an onion. He peeled off the layers of half-truths and misdirection, trying to get to the heart, and more often than not he was left holding nothing.

A knock on his door pulled Dominic back into the present. Keith called his name before he walked in. "Hey. I thought you might be hungry," Keith said as he brought in a bag of Chinese food.

Keith

Dominic grabbed the offered container of noodles. "Yeah, I could eat." They polished off both containers in relative silence. Keith didn't know what he could say to his lover at this point. It was obvious that guilt was riding him hard.

After they finished their drinks, Keith forced Dominic to finally look at him. "I know you don't believe me, but this is not your fault and no one here blames anyone but those assholes."

Dominic winced but said nothing.

"Look, asshole. Lucky has called a private meeting tonight outside the Hive. I'm going to need you to get your head back in the game."

Dominic's face was like an open book: the guilt over the deaths and even Sledge's injuries haunted him. He was about to fly apart, and his body practically vibrated with rage. He needed to either fight or fuck it out of his system. Keith decided to use that to his advantage.

Keith pounced.

Using his bulk, he tackled Dominic to the bed, pinning his arms above his head before attacking his mouth. As expected, Dominic fought against him, twisting away. He tried to fight the kiss, but Keith was ready and rode the man like an irate bull, keeping their bodies as tightly connected as possible.

This wasn't about fucking, not really. Dominic needed to burn off his anger if he was going to be effective in the field, and an orgasm was a sure way to clear his head. Keith was more than willing to do whatever he needed to pull Dominic through.

After a few bucks, Dominic started to respond to the kiss, started using his teeth and tongue to fight back, grinding his hard cock into Keith's hip. After an especially painful nip, Keith pulled back. Dominic stared at him, the tension still visible but less intense. His nostrils flared with his rapid breath as Keith swiped their lips together.

"You have to let it go. We'll get these assholes, but not if you're blinded by this guilt. We need you to focus. I need you," Keith murmured as he nibbled his earlobe. His hand slid between them as he released their straining cocks. Dominic closed his eyes as he sucked in a deep breath, held it for a few beats, then released it in a rush.

Keith spat into his palm for lube and he gripped them together tightly. He set up a ridiculously fast pace; he forced Dominic to give up control, to think of nothing but the pleasure he felt. Keith leaned back far enough to add more spit as he rubbed his thumb through their slick pre-cum.

Dominic only panted and gasped in response, and Keith made sure to keep the rhythm too breathtaking for him to form a coherent thought. It didn't take long before he was painting Keith's hand with his release. Not giving him a moment to recover, Keith straddled Dominic's chest and pushed into his open mouth.

Keith pushed his hips forward until he hit the back of Dominic's throat. "Suck it," Keith demanded and began to pump in quick stabs.

Keith threw back his head and clasped Dominic's head to hold him steady, his thrusts becoming erratic as he chased his own orgasm. When Keith felt Dominic slide his tongue across his slit, he slammed in as deep as he could as cum pumped from him.

Dominic opened his eyes and locked on to his lover's intense gaze as he swallowed. Keith pulled back as

Dominic nursed the tip, searching out every drop he could offer. Keith caressed his head, staring down at Dominic as he caught his breath.

"I love you," Dominic whispered around his hoarse throat.

Keith's heart stuttered in his chest. "I love you too, baby. Now I need you to get the fuck up and handle your shit. I've got your back," he whispered. And fuck if it wasn't true; he'd go to Hell and back and kill anyone who stood between this man and him.

As they spread out on the bed, Keith gave himself a mental pat on the back, watching Dominic's entire demeanor change as he switched gears. Taunting him had been risky, but necessary. Dominic had been withdrawing into a dangerous place of self-loathing and Keith would have done anything to pull him back from the brink.

Those fuckers had hit him where it hurt, calling into question his loyalty when not one member of the team had even considered he might be the mole. They had hoped to make the others question his loyalty by exposing that he had testified against his former unit, but it seemed it did the opposite: leaking the details of the court martial only strengthened the unit.

They trusted him and respected him even more because of what they had learned about what had happened in the hills of Afghanistan. It took a tremendous amount of courage and integrity to stand up against an entire unit.

"Are you ready to get this over with, baby?" He didn't need to ask, not really. Dominic was nothing if not a fighter; he just needed a reminder.

Dominic

The next day, they headed down to the makeshift meet area; most of the team would already be there. The armory was as secure of a location as any, if not more so: it had its own private viewing area that scanned all the camera feeds and blocked any radio signals. There was no way to tap into the video or audio feed, thanks to the special scrambler Natasha had built just for that system.

After hours reviewing the personnel records of everyone at the Hive, Lucky was no closer to finding out where the leak was. Everyone had undergone an extensive background check before they gained access; even agents that never touched sensitive information were vigorously investigated. There were no suspicious money transfers or unusual comings or goings, and everything seemed to be airtight.

"Lucky, we seem to have a camera down on the north side." Everyone stilled as Natasha punched keys on her computer monitor. "Seems we have us a sniper, gentlemen; audio confirms a single shot."

Dominic chanced a glance at Keith as everyone grabbed their gear. "There are at least twenty operators on the ground and moving towards the main building," Natasha continued as she scanned the remaining camera positions.

Lucky was already barking orders. "Okay, Shock, get a hold of the Hive and advise them of the situation. Chaos, you and Boomer grab your vests and your gear and see if you can't find a perch to take down that sniper. I want everyone on channel three; we will maintain radio contact. Everyone else, gear up, it seems they have decided to bring this fight to us." Everyone scrambled to grab their weapons.

"The Hive is aware. All operatives that are armed are headed out the back, and the Hive is now officially locked down. Washington is being notified and will have a bird in the air in fifteen." Natasha relayed the message as she grabbed her guns and knives.

I think she is excited to finally get to kill someone. For once Dominic and his Angel agreed completely.

Dominic checked his team. Everyone had the look of murder in their eyes, not just Natasha. This war had been brought to their steps. This was their home, and they were willing to defend it to the death.

It is foolish to disturb a hive of wasps.

It didn't take long to exit and make contact with the enemy; several members of the other teams had already taken on fire. Dominic and Steven immediately broke rank to head towards the garage, which was located in the middle of the firefight.

"Chaos, the alarm on the garage has been tripped. Lucky wants you and Steven to secure that building," Natasha called.

"We're making our way there now," Dominic responded.

Seems as though fate isn't such a fickle bitch after all. Maybe I'll get lucky and get to repay Sean back in spades.

Instead of disabling the alarm, the intruders had simply kicked in the door to the stairwell that led to the garage's second-floor roof. It didn't take long to locate the security breach. They weren't even attempting to hide. They'd left the door completely open, almost like they dared Dominic to catch them.

Challenge fucking accepted, his Angel mocked.

As they moved to the garage, Dominic and Steven could still hear the gun battle rage as their teammates took out the intruders. Dominic and Steven completely focused on reaching the roof and who had to be his former partner attempting to keep the team pinned down with sniper fire.

It was unclear if both men were up there, but they had to secure the roof regardless. As Dominic reached the closed door, he signaled to Steven to prepare to breach. They each turned off their headsets in case the enemy had earpieces of their own.

On a three count, Steven kicked in the door and they both laid out suppression fire as they ran out onto the roof. Dominic went left, Steven right; each man took cover.

Sean spun around as soon as they entered; one of their rounds caught him in the thigh. He lunged for cover, aimlessly spraying bullets. Dominic used hand signals to tell Steven that he would go up and around the side. Steven opened up rapid fire with two compact machine guns, hoping to confuse their prey and to draw Sean's attention as Dominic crept around the side.

His heart beat loudly in his ears as he made his way forward. Dominic had no real way of knowing if his old partner was alone. Did Sean believe both men were still pinned down, firing at him? Or was Brandon in fact lying in wait? One more corner to go. Either he was about to put down a terrorist or he was dead. One step, two steps—he waited for Steven to start firing again.

Showtime. As soon as Steven's last rounds reported, Dominic waited a two count and eased into view.

Sometimes the Gods do indeed smile down on those fighting on the side of the righteous.

Sean was leaning heavily on his uninjured leg, his weapon perched on the ledge of the pillar he was using as cover. Dominic pulled the trigger. Sean didn't even register the sound before the bullet removed the entire left side of his head.

Natasha

Natasha's cell phone buzzed, indicating another alarm had been activated. Taking cover behind the target shed, she checked to see where their defenses had failed. "The armory's roof-access doors have been breached. I am headed in that direction," she radioed to the team.

She watched nervously as Keith ran back up the small hill. "I'm headed to you," Keith radioed.

A burst of machine gun fire came from near the main building, and Natasha had to fight the urge to check on Eric. After her last transmission, Lucky gave Keith the go-ahead to fall back on her position to secure the armory. Luckily, whatever had happened on the garage was enough that they no longer took sniper fire from above.

Natasha stood near the kicked-in door of the stairwell. "Well, that is just fucking rude," Keith snickered as he walked up to her.

"You just can't get good help these days," she replied as they made their way inside. They cautiously climbed the stairs, their guns at the ready.

Natasha silenced him as they reached the roof. A shooter was in position, taking aim at someone or something. The bastard had set himself up so there was no way to get a shot at him without walking up to him. Luckily, Natasha was like a ghost.

As she made her way towards the shooter, Natasha grabbed her favorite blade. After these bastards had almost killed Sledge, she had promised herself that she would bathe in their blood. Silently she moved up, and the shooter stilled to take his shot. She quickened her steps; he pulled the trigger a fraction of a second before she reached him.

He turned as he finally heard her approach. She ran the final few feet. *Thanks for lining yourself up so pretty.* Natasha drove her boot in his face. She rode him to the ground, straddled his chest, and smiled down at him serenely as she slit his throat.

Lucky

The firefight was brutal, but decisive, once the sniper was contained. Their agents pushed forward to advance on and neutralize the attackers. Lucky moved up the embankment, approaching the garage as he engaged two combatants. He was able to quickly take them down, right before a sound from above caught his attention.

A body was falling from the roof. No, *Steven* was falling! Jesus Christ. Lucky set a land speed record sprinting across the yard. Bullets screamed past him, barely missing their mark. His only concern was getting to Steven; his younger cousin was more like a son.

Growing up in Texas and having his mother marry a black man had toughened Steven up, but the military had turned him into a machine. Steven had been Lucky's first recruit when he was picked to lead a CIA hit team, and while this job was in no sense of the word safe, Lucky had always done his best to shelter the young man.

Steven hit the ground.

"Steven, Steven!" Lucky yelled as he looked over Steven's injuries; there was blood everywhere and Lucky couldn't risk moving him in case of a spinal injury.

Steven

"Jesus... Fuck... That hurts." Steven wheezed, his voice pained and low as he heard Lucky scream his name frantically. "Hey, I'm okay, man," he groaned as Lucky searched his body for injuries; every prod produced a bloom of pain, and he couldn't hold back his yelp as Lucky opened his flak jacket to expose the bullet wound.

"Okay... All right, this doesn't look so bad, kid. Looks like a clean through and through," he heard Lucky say, although his voice seemed so distant. The corners of Steven's vision began to darken.

He opened his mouth to confirm that he had heard, but his throat suddenly wouldn't work. His mouth filled with blood, and he choked and coughed until the pain pulled him completely under.

Dominic

After their quick sweep of the rooftop revealed that Brandon was still nowhere to be found, Dominic leaned over Sean's body to check him for any communication equipment. His search was cut short as Steven screamed at him and shoved Dominic to the ground.

Dominic couldn't breathe as he moved closer to the edge; he was swimming through molasses, his steps painfully slow, as he tried to piece together what had happened.

His partner had saved his life, and in the process had taken the bullet meant for Dominic. The force toppled him off the building. Dominic rebelled at the thought that Steven might be dead; there was no way any God would see fit to trade his life for Steven's.

Steven had been hit in his side as he shoved Dominic out of the line of fire. Then time had slowed to a crawl as Dominic watched his friend's surprised expression, watched as the bullet tore through his flesh.

Steven had stumbled back with the impact, his screams echoing as he had fallen from the roof. As Dominic looked over the edge, he saw his commander cradling Steven's broken body. It looked as if he was still alive. Moving on shaky legs, Dominic headed to the stairs. He needed to see him. Dominic had to be sure.

Keith

Keith and Natasha watched in horror as someone fell from the roof of the garage. They both stood paralyzed, realizing that one of their comrades had taken the hit. Keith immediately tried to radio Dominic, and all they heard was a static noise indicating that the earpiece was off. Fear iced its way through Keith's body, turning to adrenaline as he raced towards the door.

Keith surged from the building and down the embankment; he barely noticed the firefight nearly at an end. As he drew closer, he spotted the Lieutenant rendering aid while someone screamed on the radio for Doc. He slowed before reaching them, uncertain as to what he would find. Keith couldn't breathe as he cautiously moved the few feet that separated him from the man on the ground.

Dominic

Dominic slammed through the door, his feet moving on autopilot and driving him toward his partner. His mind kept replaying the look of surprise on Steven's face when the bullet struck and the absolute panic as he fell from the roof. When Dominic reached Steven, he couldn't see anything but the blood, which seemed to be everywhere. Falling to his knees, Dominic's vision blurred as he tried to focus on the scene in front of him.

Then Keith was pulling him away as Doc rushed to Steven's side. Nausea rose in Dominic's gut as he tried to rip himself from his lover's grasp, but Keith's arms refused to budge. Dominic raged against him. Then suddenly all the fight left his body as Keith whispered, "He's alive. He is going to be okay," against his skin.

He couldn't trust anything else in the world, but he knew he could trust Keith. He leaned heavily against Keith as Doc and Lucky carried Steven on a stretcher towards the Hive. It was then that Dominic finally noticed that the fight had ceased.

Chapter 14

Dominic sat in the chair, staring at his partner's hospital bed, listening to the various machines and the heart monitor's steady beep. He had searched his whole life to find a place he belonged, and in a matter of months these men, killers all, had proven beyond measure their loyalty and friendship.

Since their first mission, he had felt connected to Steven—a kindred spirit, a quiet professional—but this went beyond that. Steven had jumped in front of a bullet meant for him, risking everything for him. Even though he only sustained a through and through, Dominic couldn't shake the fact that this man had been ready to die for him.

"How is he?" Keith's voice dragged Dominic out of his head.

"Sleeping. Doc sedated him so he wouldn't try to get up." His voice sounded ragged to his own ears as he looked at his lover.

"The stubborn bastard would, too," Keith murmured, his voice barely a whisper as he looked over his fallen comrade, as if to confirm for himself that the man was okay. "I brought you some clothes. I'll keep an eye on him while you clean up," Keith offered.

Dominic had a refusal on his tongue before he looked down to his blood-drenched clothes and hands. "Thanks, babe," he said as he tried to walk past his lover.

Keith grabbed him and quickly pulled him closer as he slanted their mouths together. The touch was chaste, fleeting, one meant to comfort.

Keith

Keith watched as his lover left the room to get cleaned up. The last year and a half had been more than he ever thought he would have with a man. Their relationship has grown dramatically from that first strategic kiss to today. Just thinking of how close he had come to losing his man strengthened his resolve to show Dominic how much he loved him.

They lived in a dangerous world, and this past week had shown them all that the dangers could come from any direction, even within. Looking at the man that had protected his lover when he couldn't, Keith couldn't help but feel a deep sense of gratitude. He owed Steven everything.

The quick death Sean and Brandon received was too merciful, but there were likely others. Someone in, or close to, the Hive had to have helped them remain undetected for so long. They were going to need to fumigate. The thought of one of the men he had fought with over the last decade trying to kill Dominic hardened his heart.

Keith was dragged from his darkening thoughts by Steven's pain laced voice. Keith's stride ate up the distance until he hovered over his friend's bed.

Steven

"Thirsty." His throat felt as if he had eaten a pound of gravel.

Damn, getting shot sucks ass.

He tried to sit up, but a whirlwind of pain put him down where he was. Goddamn, that hurt bad; the pain seemed much worse than the last time he'd been shot. Then he remembered the fall.

Correction: getting shot sucks, getting shot and then falling off a building sucks ass, he amended, grateful when Keith pushed a straw to his lips.

"Don't try to get up. Dude, Dominic will fucking kill me if I let you hurt yourself," Keith chided.

Steven chuckled then winced as the movement caused his arm to throb. "Fuck," he wheezed. "Don't make me laugh." Every breath hurt his abdomen. "Tell me we got that other asshole," he whispered, trying not to jostle his side.

Keith's nostrils flared. "That fuck that shot you? Yeah, Natasha slit his throat. She was here earlier but got called in for debriefing. She's pissed that she didn't make it to him before he pulled that trigger."

Steven cringed; he didn't want Natasha blaming herself for this. He'd have to remember to thank her later. But fuck it all, the drugs were pulling him back to sleep.

Some time later, Dominic's voice forced his eyes back open, and even though Dominic pasted on a smile, Steven could still see the pain and fear in his eyes. "Hey, brother. I see you finally decided to wake the hell up."

"Nice to see you too, asshole," he grunted as Keith left the room. Dominic was watching him closely, almost hovering, and Steven knew his friend was searching for a way to broach the subject of why he was in this bed.

"Don't ever do something that fucking stupid again!" Dominic screeched.

Well, those were not the words he was expecting.

"Okay, you want to let me in on what stupid thing I did? Because all I remember is keeping you from getting dead. Before you answer, I have to warn you: if you are implying saving your life is stupid, I will kick your fucking ass."

Steven was sweating from the pain halfway through his rant, but as he spoke his temper flared white hot at Dominic's dismissal of their friendship. He had absolutely no doubt that if the roles had been reversed, Dominic would have taken that bullet for him.

Dominic

"Fuck, I'm sorry, man. I didn't mean that. It's just..." Dominic's voice broke as he struggled to find a way to explain why what happened was fucking with him. "You're my closest friend. Fuck, man, you are my brother, and if you had... if you fucking died? I don't have the fucking words to explain what that thought does to me."

He grabbed the back of Steven's neck as he pressed their heads together. Other than Keith, Dominic couldn't think of one person on the planet who meant more to him than this man, and he honestly didn't know what he would have done if the results had been different.

"Dominic, you are my brother, and I love you. This shit is part of our jobs. Hell, this is the life we all chose to live. You know this. Don't let some twisted sense of guilt make you doubt yourself." Steven's voice was pained but strong, and Dominic could breathe again knowing his partner would be alright.

"You're right, and I do love you, so no more getting shot and falling off buildings." Dominic chuckled, in part to lighten the mood and partly to let his partner know that he was still all in. His past had come back to bite everyone in the ass.

But none of that shit mattered anymore. He'd had plenty of time over the last few hours to consider the events that had occurred, and while he wasn't certain how this game would play out, he was certain that this was his home. And he would gladly kill anyone that threatened his family.

"Yeah, yeah, you crazy bastard. I love you too, bro." Steven chuckled. "Now go tend to your man and let me get some fucking sleep." Steven's smile was at complete odds with his admonishment.

"Yeah, you need it. You look like shit, man," Dominic quipped as he started toward the door.

Keith was waiting right outside the room, leaning against the wall; his eyes were closed but the tension in his shoulders made a mockery of his appearance of being relaxed. Dominic hadn't spent much time checking in with his lover; he had spent the time his partner was in surgery pacing the halls and bargaining with God. Through it all, Keith had offered him his silent comfort and support. Now it was his turn to be the source of comfort.

Dominic whispered, "Hey, babe, Steven's nodding off. He seems to be doing okay, but he needs to rest."

"That's good, babe. He needs the rest and you look like you're about to drop. Let's go get some sleep, baby," Keith whispered back as he pulled Dominic in close.

"Yeah, let's get some sleep," Dominic said as he reached out and grasped Keith's hand. They walked in silence towards their room. Dominic knew that while they had won, there was no way he would let this go.

Somehow in the mountains of Afghanistan, his actions had set the game into motion. There were players who were hiding in the shadows, planning their next moves; attacking a CIA stronghold was a ballsy move. They had to have known that making that move would mean the entire force of the United States government would be leveled on them.

But whatever that secret was had very powerful people pulling very desperate strings. Amazingly, their crazy plan had almost succeeded. If Sean and Brandon hadn't been so focused on Dominic, and toying with him, the team might not have seen them coming until it was too late.

One thing was certain: they couldn't afford to play defensively anymore. They had to find the source of the fungus in the Hive and cut it out. With any luck, they would find out what the true crime they were paying for was. Without that piece of information, they would always be at risk of another attack.

Keith

Keith nearly ripped his clothes off before he climbed into bed and watched his lover move around the room. It was obvious that Dominic was hurting in light of Steven's injuries, but unlike before, he did not seem to be withdrawing into his head. Instead he had the look of a man whose resolve had been strengthened.

Keith was still reeling from the few moments when he didn't know if Dominic had been the one hit. In those moments, he had died a thousand deaths, and he swore he wouldn't let Dominic out of his sight again after that. The Lieutenant was going to have to team them up together; there was no other choice. Either that or he'd walk, and drag Dominic with him.

Epilogue- 6 Months later

The entire team lounged in the yard, laughing and drinking. Lucky manned the grill in his *Will Cook for Ammo* apron. Dominic leaned against Keith and enjoyed the few days of rest before heading up any new missions.

The last six months had been filled with hardships and good times. Keith had dropped in as the second sniper for Steven while he was rehabbing his injuries. The team had filled in the gaps with three trusted members from team two, Gerald, Frank, and Kevin. The new guys had blended into the team effortlessly; even Natasha seemed to accept their presence with her usual sharp tongue.

Lucky had surprisingly agreed with Keith's demands. He felt that both Steven and Dominic needed permanent spotters. Kevin would cover Steven and, of course, Keith had Dominic. Frank would work with Natasha, filling Keith's normal position as a Groundsman. Gerald was assigned to be Sam's partner, the Lieutenant and Eric in reserve. The Lieutenant wanted each man to have a permanent partner, no exceptions.

The leak within the Hive was still hidden within their midst, but with everyone on high alert, whomever they were had been forced to stay low. So the team pretended to go with the flow, not openly pursuing any leads.

Meanwhile, Natasha had installed new monitoring software and gadgets not even Headquarters was aware of. The traps were being laid, and eventually they would catch their rat. Hopefully, that would lead to whomever was masterminding the operation.

Dominic and Keith had moved into the family housing section and were planning a private wedding. Things had progressed quickly after the initial anger of having their home invaded passed. They had time to reflect how life held no guarantees, and they decided to move forward with their relationship.

Dominic

Dominic had to smile as he watched his fiancé, remembering how nervous Keith had been all day before he popped the question. Keith always had excess energy, but that day he had been bouncing around and never uttering more than one word when anyone asked him what was wrong. Dominic had been just about to ask him what had crawled up his ass and died when Keith had gone down on one knee.

"Will you marry me?" Keith whispered as he held a small box in his shaking hand. Dominic stilled, his heart jumping into his throat. Even in his wildest dreams, he had never dared to hope for someone who would accept him, flaws and all, and still love him in spite of all his wrongdoings.

But still, there he was, staring down at a man who would kill and die for him, asking him to take a leap of faith.

"Yes. I will," Dominic answered with his heart. Even with all the uncertainties still swirling around them, he knew that Keith's love was the most important, the most constant thing he had.

"Steaks are done!" Lucky yelled from the grill as Gerald carried the tray of meat towards the table.

Conversations continued to ebb and flow around him as Dominic sat and really looked at his new family. They still had people to kill to ensure their safety, and that mission would be ongoing, but for now they were safe and together.

There were still so many unknowns going into the future, but as Dominic sat next to his lover, he knew that he had found his family, his home. He had finally found the place he wanted to be, doing what he was born and trained to do.

He was a HOG, a killer who had suddenly found himself a place among a distinguished and dangerous League of Gentlemen.

To Be Continued…

Military Phrases and Acronyms

Alpha Charlie ~ Ass Chewing

ASAP ~ As soon as possible

Bird ~ Helicopter

Bol'shaya Sestra ~ Russian for older sister

Copy ~ I understand

DADT ~ Don't ask, don't tell

Digies ~ Marine Corps digital camouflage uniform

Fitrep ~ Fitness report

Five-Sided Puzzle Palace ~ The pentagon

How Copy ~ Do you understand

HMFIC ~ Head mother fucker in charge

Mladyshiy brat ~ Russian for little brother

MWR ~ Morale, Welfare and Recreation

Oscar Mike ~ On the move

Police call brass ~ Cleaning up spent casings of ammunition

RFID ~ Radio-frequency identification

SERE ~ Survival, Evasion, Resistance, and Escape

Sitrep ~ Situation report

Solid Copy ~ I completely understand

About the Author

Sharon Johnson is the pen name for a natural born story teller. The youngest of five, Sharon found the art of creating tales that had her parents often wondering if her adventures were real. Born and raised in New York City, Sharon spent most of her after school hours curled up with a book.

An avid reader from childhood young Sharon took to expanding on her favorite stories, creating fan fictions. A former United States Marine she has a quick wit and a vocabulary that would make most sailors blush. Sharon spends most of her days as an ordinary electronics technician.

If by ordinary you mean a heavily tattooed, pierced, and fiery redhead.

Sharon now resides in the beautiful Pocono Mountains with her husband, four children, two dogs, and two cats. She sets out every day to prove that you can never have too much on your plate if you love what you do. Mostly Sharon is a believer in love no matter what form you find it in.

She specializes in M/M with Alpha males who are complex and flawed but are willing to fight for their HEA.

Word of mouth is vital for any author. If you enjoyed this book please leave a review where you purchased it, on Goodreads, or post it on your social media site. Sharon spends most of her nights writing but would love to hear from you.

You can email her:

mail.sharonjohnson@sharonjohnsonauthor.com

You can find her on Facebook:

Facebook.com/SharonJohnson1979

You can Tweet her: Twitter.com/SJohnson_Author

Visit her website: www.SharonJohnsonAuthor.com

Check her blog:

http://sharonjohnsonauthor.com/blog.html

Visit her on Instagram:

www.instagram.com/sharondjohnson

Sign up for Sharon's monthly newsletter. Get sneak peeks, deleted scenes, be the first to know future release dates, first glance at cover reveals, a chance to receive free ARC's, join her beta team, and so much more!

Also Available

Beyond a Reasonable Doubt

Book 1 of the Doubt Series

DeMatteo Santiago is the Alpha of one of the largest prides in North America. He is a young, successful lion shifter, surrounded by a large family and his devoted lover. By anyone's account he has more than any one man can ask for, but his lion cares of nothing except finding their mate.

An unexpected business trip pits DeMatteo and his long awaited mate on opposite sides of the courtroom. But when challenged by ex-lovers, nosey siblings, and crazy hunters, DeMatteo realizes that finding his mate was the easy part. The real question is whether they will live long enough to be together.

This release is an M/M paranormal shifter romance. This series will contain, graphic violence, graphic language, and Mpreg. What it will not be is an instant mate fairytale, as forces set out to destroy everything and everyone.

Erasing All Doubt

(Alphas Rule)

Book 0.5 of the Doubt Series

Eighty-six thousand, four hundred seconds. One thousand, four hundred and forty minutes. Twenty-four hours. One day. In his twenty-five years of life, DeMatteo Santiago had often taken for granted how much could change in a single day.

When DeMatteo crawled to bed at 10:30 pm on May 7, 1980, there was no way of knowing how the next twenty-four hours would forever alter his life. As a young Alpha lion shifter, DeMatteo has left his pride in search of his mate and a pride of his own. But the fates have been conspiring for centuries to lead him to this precise moment in time.

May 8, 1980, 10:30 pm: a moment in time that will forever change the life of Matthew "DeMatteo" Santiago. Facing the challenges of being the new Alpha of the largest pride in the United States, DeMatteo must find a way to lead in the face of his own personal tragedy.

Where Doubt Remains

Book 2 in the Doubt Series

The story continues for Alpha DeMatteo Santiago and his mate. After the nightmare of having his pregnant mate kidnapped and tortured, DeMatteo begins the seemingly impossible process of piecing together the truth. Forces against them take this time to regroup and launch an all-out attack. Lies and half-truths fall apart as the past is investigated, but it's a race against time and failure could prove to be fatal...

This release is an M/M paranormal shifter romance. This series will contain scenes of graphic violence, graphic sex, graphic language, Mpreg, and graphic birth. What it will not be is an instant mate fairy tale, as forces set out to destroy everything and everyone around him.

Ladies and Gentlemen

Book 1.5 of The Gentlemen's League Series

Natasha Tsarsko is a CIA agent with a dubious past. She is second in command for a specialized unit of operatives that work in the shadows of organized crime.

She's built her career on capturing the worst kinds of criminals. In her world, getting close to the wrong person can get you killed. But what happens when someone she trusts wants her to risk it all?

Coming Soon

Only Truth Remains

Book 3 in the Doubt Series

Philip Cooke is the Alpha of the Montana Wolf Pack; they have served as the head enforcers for the Joint Counsel for over a hundred years mostly because of their ability to remain neutral. But when a call from Richard Santiago, Alpha Apex of all shifters in North America, summons him to hunt down a rogue lion, his options of remaining neutral disappear.

Once in Seattle, Philip meets Alpha Mate Sean and Alpha DeMatteo Santiago, nephew of the Alpha Apex and target of the rogue lion's affections. The case takes a bizarre turn when the rogue lion is killed in a failed attack, but his death leaves more questions than answers. Talk of the true mated gay Alpha had reached the pack lands, but Philip had dismissed the talks as mere rumors. Now with the undeniable evidence all around him, Phillip has to reevaluate all he has ever known and sacrificed.

When all the players are identified, one of the hunters appear to be the lost offspring of one of his own. Soon Phillip will learn that his pack is more deeply involved in this plot than anyone had ever realized, and choices made long ago have explosive consequences today. The death toll rises, but the case is far from over. In fact, it seems to be headed even closer to home.

Coming Soon 2016

No Man Left Behind

Book 2 in The Gentlemen's League Series

The trail heats up in the search for the mole hiding within the Hive, but in the game of espionage there is always another game being played just below the surface. New passions heat up and take center stage as we continue Dominic's journey to a new life.

Up and until a few months ago, Samuel Wright has never spent any significant time thinking about his love life. Although to be fair, few of his conquests spanned beyond a couple of sweaty encounters, and until very recently, he had never seen a need for more. Men, women, and everything in between, Samuel liked to think of his bed as a sexual United Nations. There was no reason to limit his options.

Well, that was true until a certain spook joined the team...

www.ingramcontent.com/pod-product-compliance
Lightning Source LLC
Chambersburg PA
CBHW071158250626
47159CB00001B/128